To Noemi and Chuck,
my dear Trinity friends —
Maybe this will inspire
a trip to Greece!
Fond wishes,
Mary Tyson Pickering
(a.k.a. Mollie)

March 3, 1985

THE MYSTERY OF THE GREEK ICON

AEGEAN SEA

The Meteora
KALAMBAKA
TRIKALA
KASTRAKI

LAMIA

AMFISSA
ITEA • DELPHI

PATRAS
SEA OF CORINTH
PELOPONNESE

ATHENS
PIRAEUS
CORINTH CANAL

PYRGOS
OLYMPIA
MYCENAE

Marty & Peter's route thru Greece to the Meteora

N
S

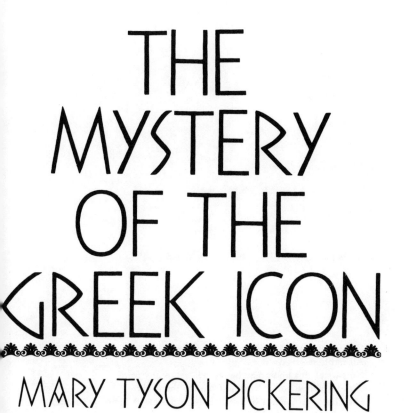

THE MYSTERY OF THE GREEK ICON

MARY TYSON PICKERING

DODD, MEAD & COMPANY

NEW YORK

Map by Salem Tamer

1 2 3 4 5 6 7 8 9 10

Library of Congress Cataloging in Publication Data

Pickering, Mary Tyson.
  The mystery of the Greek icon.

  Summary: With her only clue a small Greek icon,
Marty's search for her father, who is very ill and has
disappeared, takes her to Portugal, Switzerland, and Greece.
  [1. Mystery and detective stories. 2. Greece—
Fiction] I. Title.
PZ7.P55253My 1984   [Fic]   84–13553
ISBN 0–396–08465–6

To my granddaughter Maura
for whom the joys of travel
are still ahead

CHAPTER 1

"You're utterly, impossibly crazy, said my roommate Carol, a judgment delivered in her usual calm, unruffled manner.

"It's highly irregular," boomed Mrs. Kelly, the man-eating dean at the Salem School. "I'll have to discuss it with the Headmaster." He was a pussycat, and I thought he'd understand.

"How can you think of such a thing so close to graduation?" my Aunt Helen shrieked. She's excitable under ordinary conditions, and I'd be the first to admit this wasn't ordinary.

None of them really mattered. The crucial point, the thing that *was* important, was the message from my father. His cable lay crushed in the bottom of my shoulder bag, but the words were spelled out in neon lights across my brain:

7

HAPPY BIRTHDAY MARTY HATE MISSING CEL-
EBRATION IN SANTA LUZIA HOSPITAL WITH
PNEUMONIA PRESENTS COMING GIVE SMALL
ONE SPECIAL CARE LOVE YOU NEED YOU
TWO BART.

Beneath that was his full name and the date. The cable had been sent from Lisbon, Portugal, and arrived on my eighteenth birthday, the day I'd hoped would bring Bart himself. I'd written to him about my plan to spend the evening in Philadelphia with Aunt Helen and my two boy cousins—I'd take a bus from school and they'd drive me back in the evening. But most of all, I had wanted to see my father.

The last time I'd written to him, I'd been in a desperate mood, and I'd signed the letter, "Love you, need you so much, Two Bart," our special code name that was a call for help. After all, it was my eighteenth birthday and he'd never missed one before. I badly needed my only parent to be there.

Now his cable repeated my words but reversed the call—*he* needed *me*! Bart, that husky, handsome, healthy father, who seemed to zip across whole continents in the course of his banking business! I couldn't remember a single day of illness in the past.

I simply had to go to him. I tried to explain to Aunt Helen and Carol; I didn't try with Mrs. Kelly. I didn't even show her the cable, because it isn't easy to talk about to an outsider—how, ever since Mom died, we'd had this special thing, Bart and I, this really close communication, just when most of my friends seemed to be shaking loose from their parents.

Maybe it's the single parent bit that makes us into a special team now, or maybe it's the name Mom started using three years ago during her awful fight with leukemia. I ordinarily get "Marty," of course, but I was named Martha Barton Mickelson for both my mother and father. Mom began calling me her "Number Two Bart" whenever she was counting on me to take over some grown-up responsibility, and later, when she was very ill, my father took up the name, calling me just "Two Bart" when he especially needed me.

Now my remaining parent was sick, and he'd used that private signal. How could I ignore it?

Of course we phoned as soon as the cable arrived. Aunt Helen is Bart's only sister, and she was at least half as worried as I. But the call was worse than nothing. We got Lisbon . . . the hospital . . . the floor nurse, who spoke in stilted English. There were no phones in the patients' rooms, she told me, and *Senhor* Mickelson was much too ill to come out to her station.

I'd wept a little after I hung up, and that was when an ad I'd seen flashed through my mind: *Enjoy a week in charming Portugal! Wonderful days and nights among the fascinating sights and sounds of Lisbon*. The excursion package included airfare and hotel, and I'd remembered it because the price had seemed so little.

Spring vacation at the Salem School was only a week away, and surely the few extra days' classes I'd miss wouldn't hurt me! Even so, it wasn't easy to persuade my guardians I had to leave at once. But when I found an empty seat on the excursion flight—someone else's cancellation—Aunt Helen stopped wringing her hands, and Mrs. Kelly gave reluctant blessing to the arrangements I worked out with my teachers.

In two-and-a-half hectic days, I whipped a history assignment into shape, took a midterm math test a week ahead of my classmates, and wangled an extension for a final story in Creative English. All the while, my heart kept crying, "I'm coming, Bart! I'm coming!" and I'd have promised anything to make that plane.

"You've got a package, Marty!" Carol announced as I was cramming the last things into my suitcase. Aunt Helen would be there in an hour to drive me to the airport. "Look at all those stamps from Greece!" She studied them a moment before tossing the parcel on top of my best blouse.

But it wasn't the stamps I was interested in. This was Bart's birthday present, and I ripped it open. Inside lay a large and elegant scarf, the kind meant for draping across bare shoulders. It had a long silky fringe and a design of curliques hand painted in soft blues and yellows.

Carol waltzed the lovely thing around the room while I opened a slim package nestled in tissue paper at the bottom of the box. "Special care," Bart's cable had said, and this was certainly the smaller of the two. At first I thought it was a little book with wooden covers but, when I parted them, there were no pages, just faded religious paintings inside each leaf.

"What's that?" Carol asked, peering over my shoulder.

"It's called an icon. I saw a lot of them in the British museums last summer. Bart said they came from Eastern Orthodox churches."

"Kind of cute," said Carol. She's headed for a college major in phys ed and couldn't care less about history or religion. To be honest, I probably wouldn't have roomed with her if I hadn't wanted a direct line to her terrific brother Ken. He'd been the love of my life ever since I met him two summers ago. Big college football player, and a line that left me weak. "Kissin' cousins," he'd said when he found out I was Carol's roommate, and proved it whenever I saw him. The boys I met at Salem were children beside Ken.

Only someone like Carol would have called my icon "cute." The real ones are considered sacred: they portray holy images of Christ or the saints or the Virgin

11

Mary, the pictures often painted on wooden panels. This one was a souvenir, or so I assumed. Studying the wrapping paper more carefully, I saw markings I hadn't noticed at first: foreign words like the symbols for college fraternities; a blurry purple imprint, "U.S. Customs." For a moment, until I recalled how valuable they were, I even wondered if Bart had sent me a real antique. Anyhow, I loved my little icon, and never once suspected the importance it would have in the days ahead.

While Aunt Helen battled the late Friday afternoon traffic, she went over and over my plans. She was far more nervous than I. "I guess everything will work out, Marty. I hope so. At least the hotel the excursion package puts you in is all right—I looked it up. But remember, if Bart wants to go to Switzerland when he gets out of the hospital, you'll have to arrange your own flight to Zurich and back to Lisbon—just be sure you're there by Thursday! I do hope he'll be able to go to Lucerne. The Mullers would be so pleased to have you both. They're—"

"I know," I cut in. "She's your old school chum, and they have a hotel in Lucerne. Bart has been there before."

"I just wish I could go with you," Aunt Helen continued, and this part was for the hundredth time. "But even if it wasn't such a busy time at my office, I couldn't leave the boys." My twin cousins are thirteen and at such an active stage I doubted if she could pay anyone to stay with them, let alone ask a favor from a friend.

"I know, Aunt Helen," I said, trying to sound patient and appreciative. "You're a dear to help me. I'm just glad my 'Emergency Account' was so full of money and I had all those travelers' checks left from last summer." That trip to London with Bart had been my first big travel experience, and it helped give me the confidence to fly off to Lisbon by myself. It also meant I had a passport on hand, which made the whole thing easier.

It was a relief to settle back in the big 747. No more fuss and arguments. No more explanations. I had a window seat, and the business types next to me were too busy discussing the textile industry to try to get friendly.

While we waited for clearance, I thought how good it would be to see my father, to really talk to him. Decision time was crowding in and I couldn't seem to explain to him on paper my uncertainties about college: the two acceptances I had received balanced against my cherished dream of spending the next year traveling as his companion.

Night had fallen by the time we took off. Instead of the view I had counted on, the window reflected my urchin face. At least that's what Ken calls it. I do have a small, tipped-up nose and a pixie haircut like my mother used to wear. My dark brown hair curls a little and, short, saves me all the hours other girls spend brushing and blowing. I have Mom's gray-green eyes, but my mouth is wide like Bart's. "Poor you," he says, "no rosebud lips for *my* girl!"

I tried to smile at the face in the glass, and a strained mask leered back at me. I was excited, tired, and even a little scared. *You do what you have to do, and it won't always be easy*: Number One Principle in Bart Mickelson's code of conduct. I *had* to go to Lisbon and, against a lot of odds, at last I was on the way.

As soon as the flight attendant took my dinner tray, I put my seat in its reclining position and went to sleep. Let the other passengers watch the movie; Carol and I had seen it two months ago.

The whole plane was in darkness when I woke up. Shades were drawn across all the little windows, even my own, and the heavy breathing of the two men next to me was echoed a hundred times around the huge cabin. I was engulfed in a sea of sleep.

I pushed my shade open a crack and saw a yellow band across the eastern horizon ahead. Clouds lay below the plane like dirty powder puffs on the black counter of night. But as I watched, the yellow band spread upward and the tips of the clouds turned pink and white. How could everyone bear to sleep through such a sunrise!

Somewhere in front of us under that bright piece

of sky, Bart would be counting the hours until I arrived. At the airport, I had tried to phone the hospital again, but the circuits were so tied up, I canceled the call. Of course I had sent him a wire the day before:

AM FLYING TO LISBON   BE WITH YOU SOONEST   NOT TO WORRY   ALL MY LOVE   NUMBER TWO BART.

My best suede shoulder bag was scrunched down in the crack of the seat. I pulled it out and felt for the little icon tucked in the bottom. I'd brought it along, just as I'd packed the beautiful scarf in my suitcase. What better care could I give the "small one" than to carry it with me? Bart would tell me about it when we were together.

The icon was no more than four inches high and half that wide. Tiny brass hinges joined the two pieces of wood and opened to show the portraits inside. To the left, the Madonna and the Infant Christ stared through a heavy coat of varnish. On the right, a bald-headed old man with a long white beard and a fancy robe held a large red book. Surely not God? Perhaps a prophet or a saint.

Aunt Helen had said, "That's charming, dear. I think they sell them for souvenirs in Greece." But this really looked very special, as though Bart had selected it with care. The wooden covers were carved with delicate star-shaped leaves and tiny clusters of grapes. The pic-

15

tures themselves were faded but still held sharp color contrasts: the red of the Madonna's hooded gown, the black crosses covering the old man's robe, and the gold and blue on the cowl across his shoulders.

When the cabin began to stir with waking people, I pushed the shade completely away from my window. The sun was a shimmering ball of light emerging from the pink and yellow clouds. What a beautiful day to take me to Bart!

"Where, lady?" asked the first taxi driver I saw when I finally got through the red tape at the Lisbon airport. The Number Two Principle of Bart's code of conduct had worked fairly well: *Stick with the crowd when it's going your way; let somebody else ask the dumb questions.*

The taxi driver was a stubby, black-haired man in a shabby black jacket. I gave him my widest smile and hoped he understood English.

"Santa Luzia Hospital," I said.

"Sant' Luzia long way. We go quick?"

"Sim, por favore!" My first Portuguese words. "Yes, please," was on page one of the little phrase book Aunt Helen had given me.

The taxi swung away from the terminal and crossed the same flat, bare no-man's-land that surrounds every airport I've ever seen. At first the city looked like every other modern city, too, but when we turned away from the main boulevard, we were in another world. We bumped along a narrow street between tall, cramped buildings where every door and window was outlined with patterns of colorful tile.

We swished around a little square full of women and children, the women all in black with black scarves over their heads. Some carried shopping bags loaded with groceries, and others pushed shiny black baby carriages that made me think of the ads in the old 1910 mail order catalog I gave Bart one Christmas.

The taxi's gears ground, and we chugged up a hill so steep I thought it would reach the sky. At the top, a broader street ran past big official-looking buildings. Between them, I caught glimpses of the Tagus River far below, with more city along its banks. Then another climbing street and we popped through an opening in a long brick wall.

"Sant' Luzia!" the driver announced. "Eighty-five escudos."

I handed him one of the big bills I had received at the airport in exchange for my travelers' checks and tried a careful *"Obrigada!"* for thanks. I had arrived! Maybe Bart was even now looking out one of the big windows and watching me collect my suitcase and tote bag.

Steep steps led to a glass-fronted entrance as modern as New York. I lugged my bags across the long, airy room inside and stood in front of an imposing counter. Behind it, a young man in a severe black suit was shuffling papers.

17

"May I see Mr. Mickelson, please?" No Portuguese. Now I was here, I forgot everything except Bart.

The man looked at me questioningly. Maybe he didn't understand English.

"*Quem*?" he asked. "Who?"

"Do you speak English?"

"Some."

"My father, Barton Mickelson . . . he's here, one of your patients. May I see him, please?" My words tumbled out.

"Ah, the American gentleman! I am sorry, *menina*, Senhor Mickelson, he has gone two days ago. He was very sick, but he is better now."

CHAPTER 2

My tote bag slipped to the floor with a thud and I sagged against the counter. It had never occurred to me that Bart might already have left the hospital.

"Where did he go?" My voice quavered, struggling over the lump in my throat. "Do you have an address? Please, what about his mail?" I had sent my wire only day before yesterday, and perhaps he'd never seen it.

"If you will wait, *menina*, I will check our records." The young man disappeared into an inner office.

I took my bags to a long yellow sofa and sank gratefully into its spongy cushions. At least my father had recovered enough to leave the hospital. I could call him as soon as I found out where he had gone.

The black suit reappeared and came over to my sofa.

"It is with regret, *menina*, that I give you only the address to which we forward his mail. We have sent it to the office of the American Express. Perhaps if the *menina* inquires there, they will know his hotel."

So this was how it felt to have your heart sink. Mine went someplace below my knees. I managed to stand up and slip into my Two Bart role. *Never let it show if you lose control*, Principle Number Three, courtesy of Bart.

"I have a room at the Hotel do Rainha," I said. "Could you tell me where that is? And where the American Express office is? *Por favore?*" I *was* back in control if I could remember two of my Portuguese words.

The young man made a slight bow. "Come to the desk, please. I have a small map which will show." From beneath the counter he produced a folded map of Lisbon and opened it out.

"You are here." He made a neat x. Halfway across the map, he put another. "Your hotel is here. The office of the American Express is here." A third x. "It is not far. You may walk from your hotel, but you cannot walk from here. I will call a taxi for you."

"Thank you very much. I would really appreciate the taxi. My father was better when he left, wasn't he?" I needed one more reassurance.

"Of course, *menina*. Our *medicos* would not let him go otherwise." As he picked up the telephone, he paused. "I should also tell you, I did not give the forwarding address to the other visitor, the *senhor* who

20

came yesterday. He was not a relative. You are the daughter, and I hope you will find your father." He started to dial for the taxi.

"Wait!" I exclaimed. "Who was it that came yesterday?"

"The *senhor* did not give a name. A business acquaintance, he said. And now, good morning, *menina*." The black suit made another of its little bows.

The taxi arrived quickly but I was too groggy to enjoy the ride to the hotel. It was only 5:00 A.M. back in Philadelphia and I knew the time change was catching up with me. That and my consternation at not finding Bart at the hospital.

Thank goodness my hotel reservation was in order. As soon as the porter deposited my bags in my room, I locked the double doors and stretched out on the nearest bed. Heavy draperies covered the window, and the room was dark and cool. I fell asleep with my clothes on.

My stomach awoke me. I was starved! My watch said one o'clock Lisbon time, but what I wanted was a big breakfast. Then I'd be off to find Bart. My dear father! He might not even know I was coming. He would be in for a surprise.

Shower and shampoo were quick; you learn to do them fast at boarding school. My best designer jeans and a soft pink blouse would please Bart. It wasn't long until I was in the hotel coffee shop.

The menu was solid Portuguese, but when I looked up *"Ovos com toucinho"* in my trusty phrase book, I knew I could have eggs and bacon. A cute red-haired boy about my age took the order and served me under the watchful eye of a crochety old man in, naturally, a black suit. I hoped the redhead would get the tip I slipped under my plate.

The Hotel do Rainha was only two blocks from the broad Avenida da Liberdade, a beautiful boulevard that, on my map, bisected the city. Down the middle of the boulevard, a narrow strip of trees and flowers followed a little stream.

Heavy traffic rushed merrily past on either side of the little park. The bright sunlight, gay flowers, and the tinkle of the stream as it flowed under little wooden footbridges and popped out from beneath asphalt intersections made the whole day seem magical. I half expected to meet Bart along the way.

The magic evaporated, however, when I stepped into the American Express office. I was back in the United States, waiting in line behind a group of young men in blue jeans and whiskers. When my turn finally came, I saw why they had prolonged their inquiries. The plump woman under the information sign had the roundest, most uplifted bosom I've ever seen. A real enchantress. She directed me to an upstairs office.

"Senhor Mickelson? Ah, yes, it is here." The black-suited man was consulting his files. "His mail, he asks, will go to Lucerne in Switzerland to the care of Johann Muller."

Aunt Helen's friends at whose hotel Bart often stayed—I should have guessed. But that didn't mean he might not be spending a few days here in Lisbon before he felt like traveling. "Don't you have a local hotel listed for him, too?" I pleaded.

"That is all we have," the man said kindly. "He gave us this address two days ago. I am sorry I cannot tell you more. Let me write it for you."

"No, don't bother. I already have it. But could you help me make a plane reservation?" If that was where Bart had gone, I'd just have to follow.

"But of course, Miss Mickelson," the man said. "If you will see Senhora Veronica on the lower floor, she will help you."

A flicker of hope kept me from turning away. "Did you talk to my father yourself?"

"I did not have the pleasure, but perhaps Senhora Veronica may have done so."

Downstairs there was another line, but I was too busy chewing on my disappointment to notice much of anything. At least Bart must be well over his illness if he had left the city. As soon as I knew what flight I could get, I would call the Mullers and find out if he was with them. He had used their address on other occasions when he was traveling around Europe and wasn't sure where he would be staying, so he might be in Lucerne now or he might not.

One thing I knew: having come this far, I would keep on until I caught up with Bart or at least had a good long talk with him on the phone. The Salem School, Carol, Aunt Helen, and even the importance of my return flight had faded into another world.

Senhora Veronica was not the lady with the unreal bosom, but I liked her crisp approach as she chattered Portuguese into the phone. She flipped through my passport, made mysterious notations on a plane ticket, and told me I was all set for a flight to Zurich at one o'clock the next day. When I asked if she remembered my father, however, she shook her head. So many names and faces came each hour—how could she recall two days ago?

The row of phone booths at the back of the room was guarded by a sweet-faced girl whose brilliant lips looked as though she had been eating purple plums. I gave the Mullers' number in Lucerne and, after only a few minutes, she sent me to an empty booth.

"This is Marty Mickelson," I told the pleasant female voice on the other end of the line. "Do you know where my father is?" I couldn't stop the little sob that popped out. She must think she was talking to a child.

"Marty?" Her voice was very clear. "But Bart isn't

here, dear. He called us a few days ago from Lisbon."

"That's—that's where I am now." I got control of my voice. "I came because he was in the hospital and now he's gone off someplace. Aunt Helen said I should get in touch with you when he was able to travel because he might want to go to Lucerne and rest awhile. Now he's gone, and he left your address with American Express."

"Yes, he often does that. He was here in February but we haven't seen him since. But are you all alone, Marty? Isn't anyone traveling with you?"

"No, I just came by myself." I knew I sounded like a child again. "I have a plane reservation to Zurich tomorrow afternoon. Would it be all right if I came to Lucerne?"

"Why, of course!" said the warm, motherly voice. "I can't think of anything nicer! And isn't it lucky, our son Peter has to be in Zurich for the day tomorrow. He can meet you at the terminal in the city and you can ride out on the bus together. Do you know what time your plane gets in?"

I scrabbled for my ticket and gave it a quick glance. "It leaves Lisbon at one in the afternoon, but I'm afraid I don't know what time it arrives. I didn't ask."

"Don't worry. Just take the airport bus into the terminal and wait until Peter comes for you. He should be there by five, and I think you will be, too. And if your father calls, I'll tell him you're coming. See you tomorrow, dear." Mrs. Muller was gone.

I hung up slowly. It was almost as though a shade had been drawn to shut off a sunny day. Her voice hadn't made me homesick exactly, but I wished I were already in Zurich with only the short trip to Lucerne ahead. I'd forgotten to ask what Peter looked like but it would be nice to have someone meeting me. I'd been feeling lost since Bart had disappeared, but at least I was going someplace where they knew him and could help me get in touch.

The thought cheered me up. I smiled at Miss Purple Lips as I paid for the call. On the way to the street, I passed the information desk where I had stopped when I first came in. No lines now. The wall behind was covered with bright posters of scenes in Estoril, Sintra, and Nazaire, and I had nothing to do for the rest of the day except worry. Better to keep moving.

"I just have this afternoon," I told the Enchantress with the remarkable figure. "What can I go and see that's out of doors?" This beautiful sunny day was not one for visiting museums, even if I could have concentrated on exhibits. But my mind was much too full for that.

The Enchantress laid a colorful sheet headed "Walking Tours" in front of me and drew a big green circle in one corner.

"This is the Alfama, the oldest part of our city." Her English was good but rather stilted. "You walk easily on the cobblestones through narrow streets where no car can drive. Or perhaps you go to the castle of St. George. It is a high and beautiful place with a park and a view of all Lisbon." She added a small circle next to the big one.

"That sounds lovely," I agreed. "How do I get there?"

It appeared there was a trolley and a bus, but a taxi was not expensive. I chose the taxi because I was eager to get to the castle.

What a gorgeous spot it was! The ancient building was surrounded by shady trees, with beds of dazzling flowers and the most beautiful pair of white peacocks I've ever seen. You knew you were on top of Lisbon's highest hill because the whole panorama of the city spread out below. On one side, I could see the river and the busy streets along the docks. On another, tall modern hotels dotted the horizon. My Hotel do Rainha was tucked in among them but the distance was too great to tell where. A third side looked straight down onto the reddish-orange tiled roofs of the Alfama. I planned to walk down there later.

The castle itself was a hollow shell of high walls with a wide, bumpy path along the battlements on top. A note on my map said it had first been built by the Visigoths in A.D. 5, and the walls had withstood the violent earthquake that rocked Lisbon in 1755, ruining most of the city.

I climbed steps so steep I had to use my hands as though I were on a ladder and so narrow that I switched my shoulder bag to hang down my back. The view from the top was staggering—everything I had seen from the park below and more.

I roamed the parapet path for half an hour, ducking in and out of crumbling tower doorways and nodding to other happy visitors. I was looking for the narrow steps again when a chunky man appeared around a corner and blocked my way.

"Miss Mickelson?"

I was too astounded to be polite. How could anyone up here know my name? "Who are you?" I blurted.

"I'm a friend of your father's." He had a thick, guttural voice and shifty little eyes. Dandruff flaked the shoulders of his shiny blue suit. Alarm bells jangled in my brain because he was not at all the kind of person Bart would send to find me.

"What do you want?" I demanded as I backed slowly away. Unfortunately, I was sure the stairs were just around the corner behind him.

"I will take you to your father. I have important business to complete with him. I missed him at the hospital but I saw you request an address at the American Express."

"You saw me! And you followed me here?" I was too mad to be scared, but I would be if I stopped to think.

"Come, Miss Mickelson. You and I, we are both anxious to see him. I have a car waiting below the park." He advanced toward me, filling the narrow space, reaching out a dirty hand.

CHAPTER 3

While we stood talking on the parapet path, a noisy group of tourists had come up behind me and begun to edge past, one at a time. As they pushed by the sneaky character facing me, I slipped into the middle of the line.

The dirty hands clawed my arm but I kept moving. A step, a yard, two yards, and I was around the corner. I stayed close to the broad back in front of me as we started down the steps.

Progress was slow but, because of the narrowness, everyone had to stay in line. There was no way the Sneak—I thought of him with a capital "S"—could get to me. Halfway down, I spoke over my shoulder to the boy at my back.

"I have to get away from that man. Can I go out with you, please?"

"Why not? I even have an empty pillion on my motorbike, so be my guest!" He had a nice friendly chuckle and maybe even a nice grin underneath all those whiskers. Whiskers! I had seen this group earlier in the afternoon. These were the young men who had spent so much time talking to the Enchantress.

"A maiden in distress," he told his buddies when we finally got to the bottom of the steps. "We're rescuing her from that Greek villain up on top."

And rescue me they did. We whirled off on a half-dozen rented motorbikes, me clinging to the comforting back of Joe, whose last name I never learned. They had already explored the Alfama, but there weren't many other sights we missed in the course of the afternoon. It was dusk by the time they deposited me back at my hotel.

I turned down an invitation for the evening. I was too exhausted to sample the nightlife in Estoril, and I knew I had some thinking to do. I certainly hadn't done much, cruising on the back of Joe's motorbike. So I thanked them all, accepted Joe's whiskery kiss, and retired to the peaceful sanctuary of my room.

It seemed unlikely the Sneak knew where I was staying. In case he did, however, I ordered dinner sent to my room. I wouldn't budge outside until time to leave for the airport in the morning.

With only myself for company, all the unanswered questions of the day came out to bother me. I kept trying to imagine *why* my father would send our "Two Bart" signal and then leave Lisbon before I arrived, for gone he seemed to be. I knew he must have had some vital reason, but if only he'd received my cable saying I was on the way, I was sure he would have waited. Even if he'd left a note instead of just—disappearing!

For the first time, I wondered if I'd read his birthday message correctly. I studied the crumpled cable again: ". . . LOVE YOU NEED YOU TWO BART," the "love you, need you" written the way I'd said it in my letter to him. Odd, yes, but of course, he'd been sick when he wrote it. *But not out of his head*, an inner voice whispered. If I could just talk to him, he'd explain everything.

Maybe he would even explain the Sneak. What did *he* want of Bart, anyhow? Such an unsavory-looking man could hardly have anything to do with the bank, yet the boys had called him a Greek, and that tied in with Athens and my father's current project. But why would he be looking for Bart in Lisbon? To take my mind off our unpleasant meeting, I opened my little icon—my Greek icon. There wasn't any connection, of course—or was there? Bart *had* used extra words in his cable to ask for special care of the "small one." How confusing everything was! Maybe tomorrow when I saw the Mullers—they sounded like good, sensible people.

I was lucky on the flight to Zurich. As the plane floated through a clear, sunlit sky, the gray-haired French woman beside me pointed out landmarks far below. We crossed the Pyrenees mountains dividing France from Spain, and then the beginnings of the Alps. They grew ever higher as we flew into Switzerland.

"Genève," said my gray-haired friend, and then, "Lac Léman." Geneva and its beautiful lake. The high, jagged peaks in the distance were Mount Blanc and the Matterhorn, whose pictures I'd often seen.

"The Jungfraujoch!" She jabbed her finger toward a sharp point closer than the others. "It is not often we see this mountain without clouds!"

Soon we would be over Lucerne and then Zurich, but the plane swam into thick clouds as it began to descend.

"Will you be taking the bus into the terminal in downtown Zurich?" I asked my friend. "May I tag along?"

"Of course. But you are young to be traveling alone." For the first time, she seemed rather severe. She must have assumed I was with someone who was sitting in another part of the plane. "I will wait for you where we collect our luggage," she added.

She escorted me straight to the door of the airport bus terminal in the heart of Zurich, where the streets looked much like those of a big city back home. The traffic was just as fierce, too. Inside the terminal, benches lined a long, low-ceilinged waiting room. I chose a seat facing the door and piled my suitcase and tote bag beside me. In spite of the meal served on the plane, I was hungry again but I didn't want to miss Peter Muller when he came.

It was already past five o'clock and I anxiously examined each person who entered the door. I popped up eagerly when a short, stocky young man stopped in front of me.

"Can I be of help, Miss?" he asked in a soft, accented voice. I didn't like the glint in his dark-lashed eyes or his black mustache or even his bright pink necktie. I didn't know what Peter looked like but I was pretty sure it wasn't like this.

"Do you know my name?" It was the best test I could think of on short notice. I forgot for a moment that the Sneak had known.

"Not yet, *fraulein*. But a lovely name should go with your beautiful face. Shall I call you Marlene?"

"I'm not interested," I said and sat down abruptly. I stared at the floor as long as I could stand it and then raised my eyes to make sure he was gone. And there stood a very tall, lean young man looking down at me with puzzled eyes. This had to be Peter!

"Excuse me, but are you Miss Mickelson?" The deep voice had practically no accent at all.

I bounced to my feet, my grin wide with relief. "You

must be Peter Muller!" Not handsome, my brain was noting, but a really warm handshake.

"I've been around this room twice," said Peter, sounding somewhat exasperated. "You were talking to someone so I did not think you were the young lady I was to meet."

"An attempted pickup," I said, trying to sound nonchalant. "I'm awfully glad you're here! Your mother sounded so nice on the telephone and it's lovely to be met."

"Are these all the bags you have?" he asked. "I thought American girls always traveled with piles of luggage."

"Just shows the kind of American girls you're used to meeting!" Maybe he didn't like to be teased, but my joy at being with someone I almost knew made me light-headed.

"Let's go," he said. No smile. "The bus to Lucerne is just down the street and we've got about five minutes to make it or else we wait an hour." He scooped up suitcase and tote bag and strode out the door.

As the bus crept through the city traffic, he kept up a rapid-fire explanation of everything we passed, like a one-man guided tour. But when we turned away from the Zurich See, he stopped talking.

"The country will be beautiful from here on," he explained. "I will let you look for yourself."

The road wound between low hills and past small

homes squatting under steep roofs. Occasionally a farm appeared, big barns nestled close to houses like pictures of Swiss chalets.

The town of Lucerne was larger than I'd imagined. We followed the shore of the gleaming lake a short way, circled a small park filled with beds of bright tulips, and came to a stop beside the big railroad station.

"This is it," said Peter. "Now we walk a few blocks to my father's hotel. Later I will show you the sights of Lucerne."

I was so hungry I could have collapsed on the spot, but I scooted along beside Peter. Down the side streets, I caught tantalizing glimpses of tall old houses with brightly painted shutters and gardens full of flowers. He finally turned away from the clatter of the main street and we passed an old church with a fountain tinkling sweetly in the evening stillness.

"Welcome to Hotel Muller!" said Peter grandly as we stopped in front of two colored-glass doors. "My father's and his father's before him. And mine someday, I hope. This door is to the reception hall—the lobby—and the one on the left goes directly to the restaurant. Now we go in and see my mother."

Mrs. Muller stood behind an ancient wooden counter that crossed one corner of the paneled lobby. A brass bucket of lilacs and jasmine brightened the effect of the dark old wood. She came around the counter and hugged me like a lost daughter returning home.

"You're here at last!" she exclaimed. "Your father has told us what a healthy young thing you are, not like some of the American girls who visit us. And your aunt has written that you are as pretty as your mother! I hope you stay with us awhile, Marty."

It *was* like coming home. I felt the tears about to start so I forced a smile and said, "You're lovely to have me, Mrs. Muller, and to arrange for Peter to meet me. But I'm really anxious about my father. Have you heard anything more?"

Mrs. Muller drew back and said soberly, "Yes, we have had a note, but not a very helpful one for you, I'm afraid. He was on his way to Athens but it did not sound like bank business. I will show it to you when we meet for dinner."

CHAPTER 4

Several people were waiting by the counter, and Mrs. Muller stepped back into her role as receptionist. Peter led me to a small elevator that carried us slowly up five floors. He opened the door of a little room containing a single bed, a low chest, a chair, and a wash basin.

"It is not large," he said, "but you can see a small piece of the lake from your window. The bath is across the hall. All the family sleep on this floor and aren't far away. I think you will be comfortable."

"Oh, yes!" I agreed. "Thank you so much." I was looking at the fat comforter rolled up on the end of the bed, the down-filled "feather bed" I'd heard about, and the only cover that many Swiss families use.

"Dinner in ten minutes," said Peter and turned back to the elevator.

The meal was served at a big table separated from the main restaurant by hanging baskets of vines. Mr. Muller sat at the head of the table, a heavy man with a soft voice and eyes that twinkled even when he was serious.

"Of course we speak English!" he assured me. "And French. And Italian. Usually we use the German when we are together, but not when we have company from America. The Swiss must know many languages because all are spoken in our country."

I had already met the younger Muller children, two boys and a little girl. They were too shy to use any language at all. Throughout the meal they stared at me with round blue eyes but never made a sound. At least they had good appetites, and I joined them when it came time for second helpings.

"Please tell me more about my father," I begged as soon as it seemed polite. "I was so sure I would find him in Lisbon, and I'm afraid he wasn't really well enough to travel when he left the hospital."

"Ah, that man!" said Mr. Muller. "He drives himself when he's on business. But no one has a better time when he relaxes, as you must know. We did not know he had left Lisbon until you called. Then this came in yesterday's mail." He handed me a single sheet of airmail paper covered with Bart's jagged scrawl.

I read the letter slowly. Unfinished business in Greece, it said, and dirty business at that. Trouble with a man in the Athens office, which led to other places. The trail in Lisbon was cold when he got out of the hospital, and there were other places he must look. All mail was coming to Lucerne to be held until they heard from him again, maybe in a couple of weeks. If not by the first of the month, please get in touch with the U.S. Consulate and his office in Philadelphia. Thanks and all the best.

I looked at Mr. Muller. "What do you think it means?"

"I do not know. But your father is a careful man, Marty, and he has many friends. I do not think he would want you to worry."

Not worry! Here was Bart on some precarious undertaking, probably still weak from pneumonia, and he was telling me not to worry! I thought of the little icon tucked in the bottom of my shoulder bag.

"I want to show you something he sent me for my birthday," I said as I laid it on the table. "He told me to take special care of it, as though it meant more than just a souvenir."

"It's Greek Orthodox, certainly," said Mr. Muller as he examined it.

Peter rose and looked over his father's shoulder. "Byzantine, I would say. It looks rather valuable to me."

"But surely Bart wouldn't send Marty anything but

a reproduction," Mrs. Muller broke in. "It's a lovely thing to have but . . ."

"But it could have to do with whatever he's involved in!" Peter exclaimed with a gleam in his eyes. "I've seen some beauties in the collection of a friend, but he says the Greeks don't let the older icons out of their country any more."

"It must be a very good reproduction," said Mr. Muller, handing the folded wooden doors back to me. "I know you'll take great care of it if your father asked you to."

The meal was over and I excused myself as quickly as possible. I was so tired I couldn't see straight but I still had to do some serious planning.

It would be very pleasant to stay in Lucerne with the Mullers, but that wasn't why I had come to Europe. Everything seemed to point to Athens, even the little painted icon. I needed a good night's sleep under that lovely feather bed before I made any decisions.

Next morning I breakfasted alone at a little table in the restaurant. The kindly old waiter treated me like a member of the royal family and brought a fat, sizzling sausage to go with the steaming bowl of oatmeal. I felt well rested, and I knew what I must do to find Bart. I wanted very much to discuss my plans with Mr. Muller.

I had to go to Athens. I would call the bank's office

there first, although I didn't think they would be much help. But surely, if I went myself, *I* could find Bart, if not in Athens at least someplace in the little country of Greece. I visualized it as small and flat like the state of Delaware, surrounded by its many islands. Actually, I was right about the islands, but the mainland is a mix of rugged mountains and broad valleys, nearly the size of Pennsylvania. I should have remembered my geography.

None of the family seemed to be around the public rooms of the hotel so I pushed open the door to the kitchen. To the right was an office where Mr. Muller, Peter, and two men were discussing the next year's fuel supply. In one corner of the kitchen, Mrs. Muller was conferring with the chef. She beckoned to me.

"I must do some shopping soon. You might enjoy coming along. This afternoon Peter will take you to see the ancient covered bridges across the River Reuss."

So my talk with Mr. Muller had to wait. Even at lunch, which was the sort of hearty meal I usually enjoy, the family talked steadily about the affairs of the hotel. Afterward, I followed Peter and his father into the reception hall.

"I need your help, Mr. Muller," I began. "I've come a long way to find my father and I have this feeling that he needs me, wherever he is. I want to go to Athens and try to find him. But first I would very much like you to call his office there and see if they can tell us anything. Would you, please?"

"Hold on, young lady!" Mr. Muller sounded as stern as Mrs. Kelly back at the Salem School but his eyes still twinkled. "Running off to Athens isn't as simple as a trip into Zurich! But of course we can make the call and maybe that will settle everything for you."

Peter looked at me with speculation. I suppose he was remembering the attempted pickup he had witnessed yesterday. He seemed torn between expecting Americans to do odd things and believing American girls needed help.

Mr. Muller pulled a handsome old-fashioned gold watch from his pocket. "There's an hour's difference in time in Athens," he said. "This should be a good time to call. Come along to the office."

The phone conversation was in German. I heard Bart's name mentioned again and again as Mr. Muller apparently spoke to a series of operators and secretaries. He grew noticeably agitated as he was passed from one person to another. I looked at Peter for some clue.

"Not very helpful," he said in a low voice. "He's talked to two officials and is now being connected with a third."

Mr. Muller turned suddenly and spoke in English. "Marty, there's an envelope for you, to be mailed to your school a week from today. Shall I tell them to send it here?"

"Please, tell them I'll pick it up myself! Ask them

43

to hold it until I come for it." I *had* to get to Athens now. I was more sure than ever that Bart was in some kind of bad trouble.

"I did not like that conversation," said Mr. Muller as he hung up the phone. He faced Peter and me, and his eyes had lost their usual twinkle. "The first man to whom I spoke knew nothing of Bart. The second, a Mr. Moskonos, was almost too anxious to be helpful. He said Bart had been in the office a few days ago but has now moved on. He thought perhaps to Vienna. I felt he was not speaking the truth." He sighed as though despairing of an untrustworthy business-man.

"But the envelope—" I started to interrupt.

"Wait, Marty," he continued. "A Mr. Nikolas then came on the line. He is the head of the bank in Athens. He spoke with concern and told me of the envelope that Bart left with him. I must tell you he also said he did not think your father was fully recovered from his illness."

Those dumb tears started to come again, but I took a deep breath and made my voice steady and confident.

"There's something really wrong, Mr. Muller. I've felt it all along. Thank you very much for calling because now I will know who to see when I get to Athens." I hoped I sounded like Number Two Bart, but the lump in my throat kept getting in the way. "Could—could you try to get me a plane reservation to Greece? I have a credit card to charge it to."

"You can't go there by yourself!" Peter exclaimed. "You don't know what you might be getting into." He turned to his father. "We can't let her do it!"

"We have no right to stop her," said Mr. Muller soberly. "Even though I feel responsible, I have no authority. I would go with her but, unfortunately, I cannot leave Lucerne right now. But you, Peter—I can send you."

I glanced at Peter just in time to catch his triumphant grin. Male chauvanist he might be, but I could really use a knight in shining armor on this trip. Peter was just the person to tackle dragons and put up a good fight in the process.

Two more phone calls were necessary. One canceled my homeward flight with the excursion group from Lisbon; the other, made that evening, told Aunt Helen of my change in plans. She was so pleased to learn I'd finally met the Mullers that my next step—on to Athens—didn't faze her. Bart would be there waiting, she was sure. I wished I felt as confident.

CHAPTER 5

Peter and I left the next day. Gray skies and a gentle rain dulled the scenic bus ride into Zurich and on to the airport, but I felt warm and content with his wiry frame folded into the seat beside me. It was reassuring to see his scratched leather bag stacked by my suitcase and to hear his confident German wash away the mysteries of the airport formalities.

The flight was almost twice as long as the one from Lisbon to Zurich. There was little to see from the plane, however, because the rain clouds traveled with us.

We talked steadily, first about my school and the college plans I was reluctantly facing and then about his father's desire for Peter to study hotel management in Paris or the United States. Our families had too many plans for our futures. I dreamed of traveling with Bart while I wrote free-lance magazine articles.

Peter wanted to stay in Switzerland. Since the Swiss are known as the innkeepers of the world, he did not believe he needed the experience of training in some other country.

In some ways, he was far more grown-up than I but, in others, he seemed younger. He knew so much about European countries that I was surprised by his strange ideas about America: everyone was either very rich or very poor; most girls my age would soon marry; and New York, Florida, and California were the only desirable places in which to live. On the other hand, he spoke four languages and a smattering of others, and he professed to be afraid of nothing. A handy combination for whatever lay ahead in Greece!

By the time we arrived in downtown Athens, it was almost the dinner hour.

"See you in twenty minutes," said Peter as he left me at the door of my room. "I'll get directions to that restaurant my father told us about."

Mr. Muller had visited a Greek friend the previous evening and returned with a wealth of information about hotels and restaurants. He had also cashed travelers' checks for me and provided each of us with a large supply of Greek drachmas. But best of all, he trusted us to cope with this amazingly large and noisy city.

Mr. Muller had not discussed the painted icon with his friend. In fact, he advised me very seriously not to show it to anyone but to find out all I could about icons while I was in Athens.

The restaurant was across Omonia Square from our hotel. It wasn't mentioned in the guidebook I'd bought in a Lucerne bookstore, but neither was the hotel. Both were clean and rather new, though I had hoped for more atmosphere in the restaurant. The food, however, was wonderful: thick chewy servings of moussaka made with minced meat, tomatoes, cheese, and eggplant, topped off with a sort of almond sponge cake in a papery crust called *phyllo*.

We had a minor argument about what we should do after we ate. Much as I wanted to start hunting for Bart, there seemed little we could accomplish at that hour. I had already called the hotel where my father always stayed but he wasn't registered and the manager could tell me nothing of his whereabouts. I'd left a message, knowing perfectly well my search was not to be that easy.

Now Peter insisted we walk through the Plaka, the oldest part of the city and a mecca for all the students he had ever talked to. I said I'd rather see the Acropolis, Athens' most glorious landmark.

"Pooh!" said Peter. "You need daylight to appreciate that. Come on and see the Plaka nightlife." Which we did, of course, and spent an hour pushing our way through little streets with strange names like Mnisi-kleos and Thrassyboulou.

On the steps where those two crossed, we stopped to watch a juggler and two bearded men playing guitars. The crowd was dense, but the people looked as much like tourists as Peter and I. Music boomed from a dozen little tavernas, and the air was full of smells of beer, garlic, olive oil, and fried food. Peter tired of it as soon as I did.

On the peaceful stroll back to our hotel, he kept his arm protectively across my shoulders. He could have made it less like the act of a big brother, but I felt warm and cared for.

He was definitely the big brother next morning when we were ushered into the official chambers of my father's bank. We had asked to see Mr. Nikolas but, due to his absence, Mr. Moskonos greeted us.

Even without Mr. Muller's doubts ringing in my mind, I wouldn't have trusted this fat, smiling man. He kept stroking my hand until Peter took a firm grip on my free arm and pushed me toward a chair on the opposite side of the room.

"My dear Miss Mickelson! I never expected to see you in Athens!" Mr. Moskonos bubbled, and a skinny mustache did a funny little dance on his upper lip. "You have missed your father, I'm afraid. He talked of going to Vienna, and perhaps we can contact him there. How do you like our beautiful city?"

I started to reply but he kept right on talking. Too much? Was he nervous about something?

"You have just arrived, I know. Now what can we do to help you enjoy yourself? Ah, perhaps you and Mr. Muller would care to have dinner with me tonight? There is a beautiful restaurant—"

"Thank you," Peter interrupted firmly. "We have other plans. What Miss Mickelson wants to know is whether her father seemed to be recovered from his illness and if he left an address at which he can be reached."

"Ah, his illness! Yes." Mr. Moskonos' eyes had taken on a shifty look. "He seemed well, quite well. But I urged him to take care of himself. Now, if you will leave the number of your hotel, I will call as soon as I have been in communication with Vienna. Perhaps I can telephone by the end of the day."

I hated having to give this unpleasant man our hotel's phone number but I did want the information as soon as possible. I had one more question.

"Can you tell me when Mr. Nikolas will be in? I'd like to speak to him, too."

I missed his answer because he pushed back his chair and, as he did, a thick, brown attaché case sticking out from behind his desk caught my eye. A shiver ran down my spine as I looked back quickly to the dancing mustache. Of course all bank officials carry attaché cases, and no doubt a good many carry brown ones with brass corners. But how many would have a case with one brass corner missing? Hardly Mr. Moskonos, who looked as though he would never carry anything that wasn't in perfect condition. The shiver had reached my toes, and I felt them begin to curl.

"Then we will come in again tomorrow," Peter was saying. "Please tell Mr. Nikolas to expect us." He was standing, ready to leave. I fairly flew out of my chair to join him.

"I shall tell him," said Mr. Moskonos with that awful smile. He patted my hand one last time as he opened the outer door. "And I shall hope we have more information for you by that time. Good day, Miss Mickelson!"

Faintly, I said goodbye. I hadn't realized how dark and penetrating his eyes were. I felt certain he had seen me looking at the attaché case, and I was positive the case belonged to Bart.

"What happened to you in there?" Peter demanded as soon as we were outside on the street. "For a minute, you looked as though you'd seen a ghost."

"Oh, Peter," I gasped, "I'm sure I saw Bart's attaché case behind Mr. Moskonos' desk!"

"*Bitte sehr*! You aren't serious? How could you possibly tell?"

"It was the corners, the brass corners. Bart's has one missing. He threw it out of a train one time he almost forgot to get off and had to jump. And the one I just saw had that same corner gone. I know it must be Bart's!"

"Now wait a minute, Marty. Suppose it was. Maybe he left it when he went to Vienna."

"But we don't think he really went to Vienna. Even your father didn't believe Mr. Moskonos when he said it on the phone."

"All right, not Vienna. But wherever he has gone. Let's have a Coke or something and talk this over."

We were passing rows of tables along the sidewalk, clustered under a faded striped awning. Peter chose a table away from other customers, and a waiter brought two Cokes, cold but without ice. I'd forgotten I had to make a special request for the ice.

"I don't like Mr. Moskonos either," Peter said reasonably. "But that doesn't necessarily mean he's holding something back from us."

"He's a—" My mouth hung open. "Look, Peter! Across the street!"

We both stared. There went Mr. Moskonos, scurrying through the crowd and carrying a thick brown attaché case.

CHAPTER 6

"We'll follow him!" Peter exclaimed. But before we were even out of our chairs, Mr. Moskonos turned abruptly into the arched entrance of an office building opposite us.

We pushed our way through pedestrians crossing the wide street and entered the archway. Inside was a large marble lobby with the closed doors of two elevators at the back. Several shops opened from either side, and we peered through the windows of a pharmacy, a hairdresser's, and a travel bureau. In the end, however, we had to admit defeat; it was impossible to tell where Mr. Moskonos had gone.

"Let's set up something for this afternoon," said Peter, obviously trying to take my mind off the attaché case. "How about a tour of the city? It's a good way to see the Acropolis—and tomorrow we'll look at icons."

"Okay," I agreed. "We've got a travel agency right here. They probably have tours."

They did indeed, and we bought tickets for a city tour leaving in an hour. I wanted to hang around the lobby in case Mr. Moskonos reappeared, but Peter insisted we visit a nearby snack bar during the wait. What could we have said to Mr. Moskonos, anyhow?

The guide for our afternoon travels was an attractive black-haired girl named Vicki, whose age I guessed as twenty-five or so. Her English was good and her smile most welcoming as we climbed into the big-windowed sight-seeing bus. The next few hours were sheer pleasure.

Athens was glorious. The antiquities, as Vicki called the remains of the ancient city, fascinated me and there was much, much more to see in this twentieth-century metropolis of three million people.

Two things, however, stood out above all others. The first was a tiny church crouched in the middle of tall, businesslike buildings. We trailed Vicki down three steps and entered a round, domed room that barely held the twenty people in the group. And there on the walls were pictures very like those in my icon!

Vicki stood before a red-curtained doorway and described the religious practices of the Greek Orthodox Church and how the priests passed behind the curtain to pray. To the left of the door was a brightly painted portrait of the Madonna; to the right, the patron saint of the church. Other pictures of saints circled the room, and each bore a slight resemblance to the white-bearded old man whose face I now knew by heart.

Part of Bart's code floated through my mind: *Let somebody else ask the dumb questions*. But nobody was asking any questions about the paintings at all, so I spoke up.

"Are the pictures very old?"

"Yes, indeed! They date from the twelfth century when this church was built," Vicki replied. She seemed pleased to talk about them. "They have been repainted many times by artists who are trained to understand the colors and symbolism passed down from the Byzantine period. Today, we have men who are specialists in this type of art only. Some of them do superb work."

She turned to describe the designs on the columns in the center of the domed room. Pulling Peter with me, I slipped close to the curtained doorway and studied the Madonna. Actually, the picture was quite different from the one I carried in my shoulder bag, but the head was tipped at the same angle and was also covered by a hood. The Infant's face was like that of a wise old man.

"These are not the best examples of iconic art," said Vicki at my elbow. "There are others more outstanding in churches we do not visit today, as well as in our museums. Now please come. We must move on."

The second thrill of the afternoon was, of course, the Acropolis. During the bus trip, we caught glimpses of the huge plateau with the stately Parthenon rising from its top, but these did not begin to prepare me for the size or the majesty of the flat rocky hill that dominates the whole city of Athens.

It's hard to believe the tall, graceful columns of the Parthenon were first built back in 438 B.C. Knocked down and restored over the course of history, they still cast a spell that carries one back to the time when no vast city covered the surrounding plain and only a little village clustered below the slopes.

I was glad the tour ended at this spectacular spot. Most of the people returned downtown on the bus, but Peter and I chose to linger and soak up more of the ancient charm of the Acropolis. Before she left, Vicki singled us out as we gazed at the larger-than-life statues of Greek goddesses on whose heads rested part of the small Erectheum temple.

"Tomorrow I lead a tour to other churches and to the Byzantine Museum," she said. "You may find it especially interesting. There are never so many people in that group so perhaps we could talk more."

She was a delightful person and I hoped we might see her again. It would depend on what further information we received when we saw Mr. Nikolas in the morning.

At dusk, Peter and I climbed down from the Acropolis and strolled along the sloping path toward the city. We were hungry and not at all inclined to wait for the late Athens' dinner hour. We found an inviting taverna and ate bowls of delicious fish chowder, with a salad of cucumbers, tomatoes, feta cheese, and black olives along with thick slabs of rich, dark bread.

Back in my room, I sent postcards to Aunt Helen, Carol, and Ken. His was the hardest to write because, when I tried to picture his broad shoulders and shaggy hair, I kept seeing Peter's wiry frame and rare, warm grin. I finally scribbled a typical tourist statement with a hasty "Love" at the bottom.

The next morning, we met Mr. Nikolas. He was a fine-looking man, only a little shorter than Peter. The fringe of gray hair around his bald head matched a generous gray mustache. He shook hands warmly.

"It's a pleasure to meet you, Miss Mickelson, and you, too, Mr. Muller. I am sorry we have no word of your father yet. Here is Mr. Moskonos to tell you of his efforts yesterday." And there indeed was Mr. Moskonos, who gave us hasty handshakes and a smile that seemed sly and furtive to me.

"I called the Vienna office," he said, "but no one there has heard from your father. It is strange; I was sure that is where he said he was going."

"Thank you, Markos. Now we need not keep you from your desk." Mr. Nikolas waved him away with an authority that impressed me. As soon as we were alone, he handed me a sealed envelope.

"Your father asked that this be mailed to you next week unless he called me again. But since you are here, I believe you should have it now. Please feel free to open it."

"Thank you, but I'll wait if you don't mind." I wasn't sure I could control myself if I were to read the letter in front of anyone. Even though I liked Mr. Nikolas, the knowledge that Mr. Moskonos was in the next room made me uneasy. Better to wait a little longer to find out what Bart had written.

"Are you expecting Mr. Mickelson to return here soon?" Peter asked. "If he was going to Vienna—"

Mr. Nikolas threw up his hands. "But he did not tell *me* he was leaving for Vienna. It is too soon. And he wished especially to talk with me on Saturday. But he did not come. Monday, Tuesday, yesterday—I do not know where he is!"

He paused and watched me with concern. "We now know he has not arrived in Vienna. I have instructed Mr. Moskonos that locating Mr. Mickelson is of the highest priority. As I told Mr. Muller, your father did not look well and I suggested that he rest. Maybe he is. But we should know! I do not understand this. Perhaps your letter will tell more about his plans."

"I'll let you know if it does," I promised. "You're good to be so concerned. But since we can stay here a few days, I'm going to try very hard to find him."

Peter, always practical, said, "If we leave the city, we'll give you our forwarding address."

Mr. Nikolas nodded. "I wish you well. I will surely be in touch as soon as I hear anything."

On the way out, Mr. Moskonos popped up from his desk, where he had been making a phone call. "Miss Mickelson," he said. "I have checked and rechecked our computer. There is no word of him. Would you like my candid opinion?"

I nodded. Any opinion at all would be welcome.

"I have just remembered something. When he was here, your father spoke of the islands. He said he could use a day or two in the sun. Perhaps . . ."

"Did he mention a name?" I asked eagerly.

Mr. Moskonos only shrugged, as his phone rang, and Peter guided me to the door, muttering that he did not trust anything that man said, anyway.

I could hardly wait until we reached the same table under the same faded awning as yesterday. While Peter ordered Cokes again, this time with ice, I tore open the letter and spread its two scrawled pages on the chipped table top.

CHAPTER 7

The letter began, "My dearest daughter . . ." There followed several paragraphs of loving admonitions and reminiscence that blurred as I read them.

"It's almost as though he's saying goodbye," I whispered.

"No," said Peter firmly. "Not that, Marty. He's probably writing while he's unwell and feeling depressed."

The second page was brief. It said he was working on an unusual problem of which the icon he had sent me was an important part. "Keep it safe"—the words were underscored. "I or someone else may need it one of these days. I won't burden you with reasons now, but some of my co-workers have turned out to be not all I thought they were.

"I regret very much that I missed your birthday. You must have sparkled, the way your mother used to do. You are always in my heart." There was a postscript: "The Mullers in Switzerland have instructions in case of emergencies. Mr. M. knows what to do."

I was crying and didn't care. I handed the page to Peter and dug in my bag for a tissue. Bart sounded so unlike himself! It was a scary feeling and I felt desolate.

Peter took my hand in his big warm one. "Listen, Marty. It may not be so bad. After all, we're *here* and we're going to find him. Think how you would have felt if you'd received that letter a way off in America!"

Peter was right, of course. I really was lucky to be in Greece. Bart would say, "You do what you have to do and it won't always be easy."

I managed a small smile. "Thanks, Peter. I'm so glad you're with me. How about seeing those icons this afternoon?"

So we took another tour with Vicki. In the museum as well as in two other churches, we saw many more Byzantine portraits, some scabby and old, others freshly retouched, but none that matched my icon. Since there were only a dozen people in the group, Vicki spent much of her time with us and spoke knowledgeably about the art of icon painting. The finest icons, she explained, were done during the fifteenth and sixteenth centuries, although many are much older. In recent years, the special techniques of the old masters have been revived, and there are now a number of fine modern icon painters in Greece. Unfortunately, others work only to make money and are careless of their craftsmanship.

We also heard a good bit about the Byzantine era of Greek history. Starting with the reign of Constantine the Great in the fourth century, pagan gods and temples were suppressed and destroyed, and Christianity became the state religion. Eventually the Greeks broke from the Roman Church and looked to Constantinople, in the East, for religious leadership. Constantinople itself grew from a little village called Byzantium, which gave its name to Constantine's huge Byzantine Empire and to a period of Greek history lasting until the late 1500's.

Vicki's store of information fired my imagination and I asked far more than my share of questions. We were fast friends by the end of the afternoon but, even so, I was surprised when she invited us to her home.

"Could you come tomorrow evening?" she asked. "If you meet me at the travel bureau at half-past five, I can show you the way. My mother loves to have company, and my brother will be happy to talk about icons."

"We'll be delighted," said Peter. "Please tell me, is there a wine your mother particularly enjoys?" Dear Peter! I would never have thought of asking that. Vicki looked pleased.

We went the following day to Piraeus, the port town close to Athens. We traveled by trolley and then walked down a steep street to the curving harbor.

Our plan was to check out the boats leaving for the islands because Mr. Moskonos had suggested Bart might have gone this way. As soon as we saw the incredible number of cruise ships, ferries, freighters, and smaller vessels docked beside the long expanse of waterfront, however, we recognized the impossibility of tracing his route.

Instead, we wandered away from the busy scene and along a series of smaller harbors, each bracketed protectively by rocky headlands. At Mikrolimano, with its pleasure boats moored in long neat lines, our appetites caught up with us. Bright canopies shaded row upon row of tables set along a cement parapet, the color of each canopy indicating the nearby restaurant that served it.

We chose a table close to the water, one of several under a blue-striped roof. A young waiter in white shirt sleeves greeted us in flowery English and urged us to order the day's special. It sounded wonderful.

The salad was delicious; big shrimp, in a tangy tomato sauce, rich with feta cheese. The only problem was that the shrimp were still in their shells and the eating process was very messy.

Licking his fingers gingerly, Peter carried on a lively conversation with the waiter, who knew all the boats, schedules, and destinations for the whole of Piraeus' shipping. By the end of the meal, however, we had confirmed that we had little hope of tracing Bart.

We were waiting at the travel bureau in the center of Athens when Vicki returned from her afternoon tour. She greeted us warmly and led us into the crowds lined up for homebound buses.

At the end of a half-hour's ride, we descended into an entirely different world. Dozens of tall apartment houses rose from a blanket of trees, shrubbery, and flower beds like stubby fingers poked through a billowing, green-patterned quilt. The quiet, in contrast to the downtown streets, was broken only by the departing rumble of the bus.

We followed a curving path to Vicki's building and climbed three flights of broad, clean stairs. Mrs. Nakrodis, a matronly woman with a thick coil of white-streaked hair adding inches to her height, met us at the door of the apartment. Although she spoke little English, her smiling brown eyes followed every word we said. She showed her approval with broad smiles and frequent exclamations of "Yes! Yes!"

Mrs. Nakrodis grasped our hands and led us through a short hallway into a living room whose small size was extended by glass doors opening onto a little balcony. Beyond, the billowing green canopy of treetops obscured the neighboring apartments. The room's white walls were covered with large photographs mounted on mats of green, red, and gold. The furniture was low and contemporary in the style I had always thought Scandinavian, not Greek. Its light wood and muted colors allowed the photographs to dominate.

"My brother Stephanos will be here any minute," said Vicki. "These are his photographs. It is his hobby to take pictures and he travels to all parts of our country to do so."

Peter offered the brown-bagged wine bottle to Mrs. Nakrodis. "I brought this for you."

"Yes, yes!" The eager smile beamed. She took the bag to another room and returned with a tray of small glasses and a slender decanter.

"This is ouzo," said Vicki. "Have you tried it?"

"Not yet," Peter replied. "We've been waiting for an occasion. It's your country's favorite liqueur, I believe?"

"Indeed it is. It is flavored with anise—to you it will taste like licorice." She poured a little in each glass.

"Go easy," Peter muttered to me. "Ouzo is potent stuff."

How right he was! My first sip was almost more

65

than I could manage and burned my throat as I tried to swallow. But the aftertaste was sweet and tingly. I looked at Peter and he winked. I had told him I rarely drank even wine, and then only if it was sweet and smooth.

Vicki passed a plate of small pastries and little brown lumps. "Dolmathakia," she said of the lumps. "To you, they are stuffed grapevine leaves. They are filled with rice and currants and chopped onion."

The stuffed leaves were cold and tasted very strange, but the pastries were crisp and cheesy. Thank goodness my stomach was adaptable!

"We use phyllo for the pastry," she continued. "In these, there are feta and Gruyère cheeses. Do you like them?" It was easy to agree as each warm bite melted in my mouth.

"My greetings to our visitors!" exclaimed a voice from the hall. Into the living room strode a stocky young man with a beautiful smile.

"Stephanos!" said Mrs. Nakrodis and added a rush of words in Greek.

"Our visitors are Miss Mickelson and Mr. Muller," Vicki interrupted. She turned to me. "This is, of course, my brother."

Stephanos came straight to me. As he bowed over my hand, I half expected a courtly kiss, but he only squeezed it gently. His large dark eyes were so close

66

to my face I could have counted the long, black lashes.

"It is a great pleasure to have a lovely American visit us," he said so sincerely that I believed every word. He moved to Peter and shook hands in such a man-to-man fashion that he made one forget he was several inches shorter. "Ah! I see you are sampling the ouzo. You must never add water, you know—no ice cubes! It turns at once to milk."

"Please excuse my mother and me," said Vicki. "We must fix the dinner."

"May I come?" I was eager to see the kitchen and learn more about Greek food. So for the next hour, I perched on a high stool and watched the meal take shape: the baked fish, fresh peas and artichokes cooked with onion and olive oil, and a spinach salad that included so many items I lost count.

When we finally gathered in the dining room, Mrs. Nakrodis was perspiring slightly, and the air was filled with spicy odors. Everything was delicious. We all ate heartily, with a lively conversation punctuated by our hostess' happy "Yes, yes!"

We soon moved to a first name basis and Stephanos became a friendly Steve. As Vicki rose to clear the table, he asked, "But you are not here in Greece strictly for pleasure, I think?"

"No," I said. "I'm trying to find my father. He's associated with a bank." I gave its name. "But he has been ill and they seem to have lost track of him. We think he has left Athens, but we don't know where he has gone."

"Well, there are many places in Greece beside Athens." Steve smiled. "I have been to every corner of our country. Perhaps I could help in some way."

I looked at Peter. My instinct was to trust this friendly family, and we certainly could use some help. His reassuring nod convinced me.

"My father is investigating something that seems to be connected with someone in his bank," I explained. "He went to Lisbon and then said the trail was cold. The last we knew, he came back here and disappeared. We don't know where to go next."

"Perhaps Thessalonika?" Steve suggested. "It is another large city in the north."

"Marty," said Peter, "I think perhaps you should show them your icon."

"You have an icon?" exclaimed Vicki. "I knew you were interested in them but I did not know why."

"I'll get my bag," I said, excusing myself from the table. In a moment I was back and handing the little icon to Steve.

"It's a beauty!" he asserted as he opened it. His heavy black brows shot up, and he turned quickly to pass it to his mother. She spoke excitedly in Greek, calling Vicki to her side.

"Marty," said Steve, "this icon is a very fine piece of work. It is hard to believe it is a modern-day reproduction. Whether it is or not, we can tell you where it comes from. The paintings are like those in a monastery near the home of my mother, in a place called the Meteora."

CHAPTER 8

"You recognize it!" I shouted. Then I blushed. "I'm sorry, I didn't mean to be so loud. But that's wonderful!" I grinned at Peter, who looked as pleased as I was. "Do tell us about it."

"The Meteora!" exclaimed Vicki. "We do not see artifacts from those monasteries here in Athens." She was serving us small squares of baklava, that rich, sweet dessert full of nuts and honey. "The Meteora is a group of monasteries near Kalambaka, an unusual place where each monastery rests by itself upon a high rock. In the old days, they could only be reached by nets and ropes and ladders. Our mother comes from the valley of the Pinios which flows below the rocks."

"Yes, yes!" agreed Mrs. Nakrodis, beaming on all of us.

Peter, always my practical partner, asked, "Can we go there? Is there a bus?"

"Of course," said Steve. "But it lies more than three hundred kilometers to the north, perhaps two hundred of your miles. There are hotels in Kalambaka, and you would want to stay one or two nights."

Mrs. Nakrodis spoke urgently to Steve. He listened and turned to me. "She says the portrait in your icon is of St. Nikolas, the patron of a monastery no longer in use. She believes only six are still open. She wants me to say she hopes you go to Meteora because it is one of the most beautiful sights in all of Greece."

"Yes, yes!" Mrs. Nakrodis nodded emphatically.

"We could go tomorrow," I said. "Is there a bus on Saturdays?"

"There are many buses to Trikala," Vicki explained. "From Trikala, there is another bus to Kalambaka. I am sure it runs every day. The trip will take about six hours."

Steve had been looking thoughtful. "I have a better idea," he said, a happy gleam in his dark eyes. "Since tomorrow is Saturday, my office closes at noon. I will drive you there and return on Sunday. I will enjoy watching you when you first see the rocks of Meteora!"

"That would be great, Steve," said Peter. "There is so much I want to ask about Greece."

"And this is my weekend to work," Vicki groaned. "I wish I could go with you."

By the time we left the Nakrodis apartment, plans had been made for Steve to pick us up at our hotel the next afternoon. Vicki suggested that we check out of our rooms and reserve them again in four days' time, which would allow for visiting the monasteries and traveling back to Athens by bus.

"You might decide to go on to Delphi," she added, "and in that case, you could always call your hotel. At least you wouldn't be paying for rooms you weren't using." Vicki was a very practical young woman.

I was amazed at how my perspective had changed. Delphi of the famous oracle was a place I had always dreamed of seeing but now, believing my father was somewhere in Greece, I wanted only to find him. Delphi might come later but it seemed unimportant at the moment.

While Vicki helped her mother, Steve accompanied us to the bus stop and gave careful instructions about where we should get off. There were few other passengers on the rumbling trip back into the center of the city, but the downtown streets were still full of people. As we walked the last blocks to our hotel, my hand felt warm and secure in Peter's friendly grip.

"We're lucky to have come across someone like Steve," said Peter as we strolled along.

"We sure are," I agreed enthusiastically. "He's awfully nice!" I felt the hand holding mine tighten and then go slack. Now what did that mean? Could Peter, brotherly Peter, be jealous?

When we stopped at the hotel desk for our keys,

the clerk handed Peter a note. Mr. Muller had telephoned and wanted to talk to him as soon as possible.

"I hope there's nothing wrong at home," Peter said. as he asked the clerk to place the call.

We went up to our rooms and, in about twenty minutes, Peter knocked sharply at my door.

"Marty!" he exclaimed, dropping into the room's only chair. "Your father phoned Lucerne! But it was a very strange call—my father says they were cut off in the middle of a sentence. He kept waiting and waiting for him to ring back, but nothing more came through."

"What did he say?" I could hardly believe someone had spoken to Bart *today*. I felt a wild surge of joy.

"He said, 'Johann, I need help. Something more than the trail of the torch starts here. Tell . . . ' and that's when they were cut off."

"And he didn't call back? That's so weird!"

"It was as though someone grabbed the phone. My father said Bart was almost whispering, and then there was a loud sound in the background just before the line went dead."

"What do you think it means, Peter? Where was the call from?" My joy had been short lived.

"My father was fairly sure he heard a Greek operator when the call was coming through, so he checked and was told it had been routed through Athens."

"The Olympic torch begins at Olympia," I said

73

slowly. "That's in southern Greece somewhere. It's our first real clue and it sounds like he's in trouble. I think we should go, Peter!"

"But Steve is driving us to Kalambaka tomorrow."

"Perhaps he would take us to Olympia instead." Finding my icon's home could wait—it was Bart who needed me!

We had no way to get in touch with Steve; we knew neither the name of his office nor his phone number there. But when he arrived the next afternoon, he must have seen as soon as he jumped down from his battered van that something had happened.

"My friends! You have had bad news?" he asked as he looked at our sober faces.

"We had a message from my father," I blurted without even saying hello. "Is it possible for you to take us to Olympia, Steve?"

"You do not want to go to Kalambaka?" he asked, staring at us as though he had misunderstood. "The message, how did you receive it?"

Peter explained. He said we realized that Steve might not want to take us to Olympia but we felt we should go there as quickly as possible.

"Olympia is not a problem," said Steve, setting our bags in the back of the van. "It is about the same distance but it is to the south, on the Peloponnese." He pronounced it "pea-low-pa-knees," and it took me a moment to recognize the name of the jag-

74

ged peninsula that lies beyond the Gulf of Corinth.

"Oh, thank you!" I said, the tears trying to surface. "That cut-off message sounded so urgent and so strange! I just wish we knew what else he meant to say."

"We will consider the possibilities as we go," said Steve. "It is a long trip and now we must start."

He helped me onto a little jumpseat where I could look ahead between Steve's broad, solid shoulders and Peter's higher, bony ones. The van's gears ground and we rocketed into the surging traffic of Omonia Square.

Saturday afternoon was the time for every car in Athens to be leaving the city, and the traffic was tremendous. Peter and I sat silent and prayerful as Steve maneuvered his way through miles of clogged streets, creeping one minute and zooming ahead the next. It was almost an hour before we were clear of the city and moving smoothly along a broad highway. Ugly industrial plants were interspersed with clusters of small houses and, off to the left, we had more and more frequent glimpses of the blue Aegean Sea.

Steve picked up the conversation as though he had been thinking of nothing else. "Your father—you call him Bart?—is following a trail, you said. You think it has taken him to Olympia, where the ancient games were held. Now whom would he want told?"

"He wrote to Peter's father earlier that he should tell the American Consulate and Bart's office in Philadelphia if he didn't hear from Bart by the first of May. But that's still over two weeks off."

"His investigation may have speeded up," Peter suggested. "At least, it sounds as though he needs help *now*."

"I would not think you have enough information to ask for help from your government," Steve said. "Bart does not know Marty is in this country looking for him, and he may only have been asking that she be told."

What Steve said was true: we really had very few concrete facts. Yet everything added up to Bart's needing help. My encounter with the Sneak on the castle wall in Lisbon seemed dim and unimportant compared to Mr. Moskonos and the attaché case I was sure belonged to Bart. But even the unfinished telephone call provided little to back up our suspicions.

"He could have meant 'Tell the police' or 'Tell my office'—but which one?" I pondered. "He might have meant Mr. Nikolas in Athens or the bank back home. But you're right, Steve, he could have been sending a message to me."

Presently we crossed the Corinth Canal, a deep, spectacular slice through the narrow neck of the Peloponnese peninsula. For awhile longer, we followed the main road, passing close to the ancient ruins of Mycenae. Soon Steve pulled into a tiny restaurant and led us to its canopied terrace. At iron tables, we drank sugary orange juice and ate cheese and crusty rolls.

"We still have a long, rough ride," he said. "From here, we will take smaller roads across the mountains. We should be in Olympia before the sun sets."

The sun had already disappeared when we reached the little town of Olympia, a village that has mushroomed to serve the tourists who come to visit the site of the ancient games.

"There's a youth hostel here," said Steve, "but, if you agree, we will go to the house of my father's cousin. She has three rooms for guests and will give us breakfast, all for a very few drachmas."

Mrs. Papagoris welcomed us and made businesslike arrangements with Steve. Her plastered house stood like a square white box on a graveled side street that climbed above the village. She led us up steep outside stairs to the second floor, where our rooms opened onto a shallow balcony.

A large corner room with three beds she assigned to Peter and Steve. Mine was next door, small and bare but shiny clean. Across the inner hall were the bathrooms, one containing only a tub, the other a toilet and wash basin.

"She says tonight we will be her guests for dinner," Steve told us, his eyes twinkling. "I guess I don't come very often. Tomorrow, only breakfast. The other room up here is let to two schoolteachers. We all share the facilities. I hope it's all right, Marty?"

"It's great!" I said. For the small price, it was more than I had expected. I went out on the balcony and looked across the rooftops toward a huge hotel on the opposite hillside. Its lights already shining, it dwarfed the houses in the village below.

"Steve!" I called. "What is that over there?"

He appeared on the balcony. "That's the most famous hotel in the Peloponnese, and the most expensive. But you should go there for a drink and see the flower gardens."

The dinner Mrs. Papagoris served us was fit for a king, let alone a cousin who dropped in with two friends. There were shishkebabs; a huge bowl of rice speckled with slivers of olives; and, to wash it all down, a fruity and fragrant wine from a big jug in the kitchen.

Mrs. Papagoris had a sad, seamed face. Her husband was dead and her sons married, living in Athens. The young girl who helped her, a granddaughter, smiled shyly whenever I caught her eye, but most of her attention was for Steve. He kept us all laughing with his gay banter, sometimes in Greek and sometimes in English, while his two relatives treated him as though he were a Greek god come back to earth.

Steve left the following morning, promising to return the next weekend if we were still in Olympia. Since we had little idea how long our investigation might take, he mapped out the return trip to Athens by bus and gave us his phone number.

CHAPTER 9

Although the village had taken its name, the ancient Olympia was never a town. It had been a religious sanctuary dedicated to the old Greek gods of mythology. The ruins, now partially excavated, contain temples and treasure-houses as well as the parade grounds, stadium, and other structures related to the original Olympic Games. The Games were first held in 776 B.C.; for more than a thousand years, they were repeated at four-year intervals and then abandoned by a Roman emperor who considered them pagan rituals. In 1896, the Games were begun once more but not at Olympia, where the site had long since been demolished by man and nature.

Today one walks beneath tall old trees, among partially reconstructed walls and chunks of old columns scattered among the wild flowers. The stone-lined pas-

sage to the playing field no longer has a roof, but anyone passing beneath the keystone arch at one end still
feels the presence of the hot, triumphant athletes who
once charged out into the broad stadium.

All this awaited us as Peter and I paid our entrance
fee to a crinkled old woman in rusty black at the little
ticket booth. Her dark, beady eyes gleamed as she offered an English guidebook with our tickets.

"For English, it help understand. You like?" Her
withered old hands flipped the pages.

Peter and I exchanged winks: we were American
and Swiss. Still, it seemed a good idea.

"Do many Americans come here?" I asked curiously.

"Ah, American! Yes, yes, many. You are very pretty
miss, and thank you!" I handed her the extra drachma
and took the book.

I loved Olympia. In one part, the tall columns had
been rebuilt and outlined the site of a wrestling arena.
In other places, huge drumlike chunks of stone lay
in sequence on the ground like the bones of some gigantic skeleton. Low walls outlined the eighty rooms
of a posh hotel site for visiting dignitaries, and I pic-
tured the flowing robes that once trailed through its
porticos.

The bleakness of many ruins was missing in Olympia because tall, elegant Mediterranean pines cast shade
and color across the ragged columns and piles of excavated rock. A little group of tourists was gathered

around the site of the sacred Olympic flame; I moved near enough to hear the guide explaining how, although nothing burned there now, the flame was re-kindled with rays from the sun each time a torch was to be carried to one of the modern games.

Presently Peter and I explored the narrow passage through which the Greek athletes had entered the vast Olympic playing field. We passed under its single re-maining arch and between the smooth stone walls out onto the grass-covered banks of the stadium. Here doz-ens of visitors roamed the field or sat on the steep side-slopes which long ago had held rows of cheering spectators.

"Mind if we go clear around?" Peter asked, almost shyly. "It is an ambition of mine."

"I'd rather not." It looked hot, flat, and uninterest-ing. "Meet you by the gate in half an hour."

Returning through the stone passage, I wandered along the Street of Heroes where empty pedestals had once held statues honoring the winning athletes. Near the entrance gate was a huge drum-shaped rock from which I could watch the people streaming in and out of the grounds. It was easy to clamber up.

My perch was shady and peaceful; I was an invisible observer, a small bump hidden by the shadows. Over-head, the dark pine boughs whispered and sighed, while below, gaily-dressed tourists straggled past. I knew there was little chance that Bart would be among them, but Olympia had cast its spell: in a place like this, anything could happen.

I thought about Mr. Moskonos, that furtive and disturbing man in Athens with his neat dark suit and dancing mustache. He came so sharply to mind that it was a few minutes before I realized I was seeing several of his brothers on the path. A small clot of four black suits went by, then two, and now a single man, all dressed the same and certainly unlike the other tourists.

So many somber men seemed odd, but perhaps they were attending a conference. Did people hold conferences at Olympia? A long line of laughing high-school students was trailing toward the gate. Behind them came Peter, beckoning wildly.

I jumped down onto the path and he grabbed my hand, sweeping me back the way he'd come. "There's something you've got to see! I'm not sure what it means, but it's back in the tunnel—the passage to the playing field. I just noticed it in the sunlight."

A tunnel it may have been long ago, but without its roof, it lay open to the sky and sun, every stone revealed now in the strong light of noon. Peter squatted on his haunches, pulling me down beside him. Without a word, he pointed to the wall.

B . . . A . . . R . . . t—faint, shaky lines traced across the lowest course of stones! Two or three blank surfaces separated each letter; the *B* was fairly sharp, the others less so, the small *t* barely visible. But it was there—Bart's name—and nothing could be less Greek than that!

I ran my fingers over the surface and they came away smudged. "Blood!" I gulped.

"No, charcoal," said Peter. "I even found a little piece."

"There's the sacred flame." I was thinking out loud. "Weren't there some bits of charred wood around that?"

The round basin had been brushed clean, ready for a new flame to be lighted, but there were indeed small pieces of burned wood in the deep grass. Someone could find them if he looked, or if he were sitting on the ground.

"Peter, suppose Bart was tied up and whoever was carrying him propped him by the basin while they stopped to rest? If his hands were free, he could have picked up a piece then." The idea made me shiver.

Peter nodded. "They could have stopped to rest in the passage, too, or if they were carrying him—one his feet and one his shoulders—his hand would have been just about level with those letters."

"But there'd have been other people around. Even if they said he was ill . . ."

"Well, however he did it, at least he managed to leave a clue. Your father's a brave man, Marty. I think we must be getting close." His arm went around my shoulders and I crumpled onto his chest. But this time I didn't cry. There was too much we had to find out, and I knew we must do it quickly.

"We'll have to get some lunch," said my ever practical knight. "Then we can search the whole place this afternoon, even though it looks too public for anyone to be hiding."

We stopped at the ticket booth by the gate and asked the sad old woman if we could have passes to come back later.

"Ah, many do," she said. "Those vultures from the hotel, they ask passes for the night, too. But nobody gets in after dark."

"You mean those men in business suits?" I tried to sound casual. "Who are they? Archaeologists?"

"Not them! Nobody you should know, pretty miss. Two days they come, and never a guidebook or question about the Games. Their minds are too full of money and merchandise." As she started to turn away, she muttered, almost to herself, "Even when one is too ill to walk alone, they argue with one another."

Before I could even open my mouth, Peter picked up on what she had said. "One minute, please," he blurted. "You say, an ill man? Did they take him in or bring him out?"

"In. I did not see them return." She scowled, motioning to a new group waiting for tickets. "No business of mine nor yours, either. I talk too much."

"I saw about ten of them, Peter!" The words tumbled out now. "They all looked like the men in downtown Athens. The sick man must have been Bart!"

"There's a word for you, Marty," said Peter, breaking into his rare and charming smile. "Is it grasping for hay?"

"No, straws. But we're looking for anything that's not normal—"

"I think it is possible. If they were meeting others and Bart was essential to their business, they could well have dragged him along. But did they leave him inside?"

Hungry as I was, lunch was only something to get out of the way. We gulped food at a nearby restaurant and returned as quickly as possible to Olympia. But during the afternoon, as we explored every corner of the ruins, we found nothing more to show Bart had been there. Hot, tired, and discouraged, we went back to the little town and our rooms in Mrs. Papagoris' house.

"Give you an hour," Peter said. "Then let's go up to that big hotel and see how the other half of the world lives."

"You want to take my mind off Bart," I said glumly. "But all right, we might as well."

A bath and my lavender suit did wonders for my spirits, and the sight of Peter in crisp navy sports shirt and sharply creased cord slacks made me feel I was on a special date with my best beau. Romantic he was not, however—just cheerful and friendly. Why should I expect anything else?

We walked down through Mrs. Papagoris' vineyard and along the main street to a paved driveway winding up the opposite hillside. Roses climbed the walls bracketing the smooth, steep drive, and the evening was filled with their scent.

The walls ended abruptly and the driveway circled gracefully to the entrance of the palatial hotel. Within the broad curve, shadowy couples strolled through a fragrant garden.

We found the outdoor terrace and chose a table by the low balustrade where we could look over the village and the whole valley beyond. Lights twinkled below us, and the darkness where they ceased was the ancient Olympia. As we sipped our wine, I slipped my hand into Peter's and felt a warm, responding squeeze. A special date indeed!

Suddenly Peter's grip became so tight it hurt. "Don't turn—just listen!" he whispered.

I realized there were voices coming from a table at our backs, deep rumblings to which I had been paying no attention. I began to catch occasional phrases in English. Someone was translating parts of the Greek conversation for someone else.

" . . . go to Kalambaka for the merchandise," I

heard. "Don't worry about the man. We take him too. He is no problem while he sleeps."

Shivers ran along my spine like icy fingers playing a macabre tune. I was rigid from the effort of not turning to look, and I could feel the intensity with which Peter was listening. First, there was "the man"—could they mean Bart? And secondly, Kalambaka was the town below the Meteora, from which Vicki's mother had said my icon came.

Three different voices seemed to be arguing in Greek. Then came the English: "Only Demetrius, you, and I go to Kalambaka. It is too noticeable for more. We leave tomorrow. In two days, Markos will meet us with the papers."

More Greek and the clink of glasses. " . . . be easier to lose a body in the mountains. Don't worry, Thomas, the ravines are deep. We'll take care of him . . . "

The icy fingers became sharp icicles stabbing at my heart. Could those voices be talking about my father?

Chairs scraped, and the word "dinner" caught my attention. I turned casually in time to see dark-suited backs moving toward the door at the rear of the terrace.

CHAPTER 10

"We have to see who they are!" I exclaimed in a shaky voice. "I'll go inside as though I'm looking for the ladies' room and try to get a look at their faces."

"We'll both go inside," said Peter, "as soon as I've paid the bill. Try to look calm and relaxed, Marty."

Relaxed? I was trembling almost too much to stand up. Somehow I managed to follow Peter's tall figure to the back of the terrace and into the hotel's elegant lobby.

"Wait for me," he directed and strode confidently toward the tubs of flowering white shrubs that guarded the entrance to the dining room. He addressed the austere doorman and stepped inside.

In a few moments he was back. "There's a balcony all around the room. We can probably get to it from the next floor."

"But what did you tell the man at the door?"

"I just said I wanted to see if my party had arrived yet. He let me look around, but the men we're after were all the way across the room and I couldn't see very much."

A broad stairway rose gracefully at the other end of the lobby. We ascended, in what I hoped was a leisurely manner, to a lounge lined with shelves of books and magazines. Beyond, a narrow hall led to a row of doorways draped with red velvet. The heavy curtains were looped back to give access to a shadowy balcony packed with tables and chairs. At the height of the season, this too would be used for diners.

We felt our way through the gloom to the low railing and looked down on the ornate dining room below. Dazzling white cloths were dotted with colorful bouquets of flowers. An army of waiters darted among the tables, trays of food balanced like giant Frisbees on their fingertips.

The occupants of only one table matched the group we were looking for. Every other table of four had at least one woman or child in the party. Ours was almost directly below where we stood, and we had a fine view of the tops of their heads. There was one man with rather long sandy-brown hair and the glint of glasses perched on his brow. The crowns of two others were thick and black, one shining with hair cream. The fourth head was bald but with bristling eyebrows and tufts above the ears.

Peter chuckled. "Good detectives would have some marvelous listening device for an occasion like this, but I'm afraid *we're* out of luck."

"Even if we could afford to go down there and have dinner, we couldn't get close enough to hear anything," I said. "Let's wait in the lobby till they come out."

"We'll starve! But you're right. We need a good look at them, especially the ones we'll be following to Kalambaka."

"You agree we have to go there next!" I sighed with relief. I had expected to have to argue the point. "Let's get out of here before somebody notices us."

We groped our way back to the hall and descended to the lobby. Dozens of sofas and deep chairs were arranged in conversation groupings, and we settled ourselves in an inconspicuous corner facing the entrance to the dining room.

"It may be a long wait," said Peter. "Try and look happy, as though you enjoy my company."

"But I do, Peter! I couldn't do any of this without you!"

"We'll have to call Steve," Peter continued, ignoring the compliment I had intended. "He can meet us in Kalambaka next weekend, but I think *we'd* better get there as soon as we can."

"Do you think Bart is here in this hotel?" I tried to smile as three women emerged from the dining room and looked at us curiously.

"He could be. But he could be someplace else in the town, too. . . . You're doing fine, Marty."

"Somehow, I feel he's right here. But if he is, why would they have taken him to the ruins?"

"Marty"—Peter took my hand—"you do understand they probably are keeping him drugged, don't you?"

"I'm trying not to think about that. I just know we've got to find him as soon as possible."

We sat silently, busy with our private thoughts. My hand was still in Peter's and it felt good to know he was with me in this. From time to time, diners wandered into the lobby, but it was a long while until we saw the men we were watching for. My stomach had begun to rumble embarrassingly when they finally appeared.

Still speaking rapid Greek, they passed close to us on their way to the cigar counter beside the elevators. The sandy-haired man wasn't talking; he would be the one they addressed in English. Skinny, with wire-rimmed glasses perched on a hawklike nose, he was the only one in a brown suit.

The bald head and bushy eyebrows wore horned-rimmed glasses. He was the tallest of the four but he walked with a shambling stoop. The other two could have been twins of Mr. Moskonos with their straight black hair and small mustaches. They talked with their hands and their eyes, and the greasy-haired one stopped almost beside us to blow his nose in an unpleasantly noisy manner.

We watched them buy their cigars and move slowly to the elevators. Peter pulled himself out of the deep chair.

"Might as well ride up, too," he said. "You stay here, Marty." Before I could protest, he was halfway across the broad room. But he wasn't quick enough; the elevator doors slid closed in his face. He stood there a few minutes and then came back to me.

"They went to the third floor—that's the top," he said. "The directory says the third is private suites, so it's just as well I didn't go up. It would have been too obvious."

"Peter, should we go to the police now?" I had been turning over in my mind the facts we had, and they seemed to me very persuasive.

"It's a—what, a shake-up?" Peter began.

"Toss-up," I said automatically.

"Yes, well, a toss-up whether what we know would stand against what three 'respectable' Greeks and an Englishman staying in this luxury hotel would say to the police. Steve might put it across, but I don't know if we could. And if we couldn't get the police to help, we would have let the men know we're on their trail. I'm not sure—what do you want to do?"

"Oh, dear!" I thought about the danger Bart could

be in right now, here in Olympia. "We do need Steve! Let's call and ask *him*!"

"Not from here," said Peter. "It would be safer to go down to the village and find a phone."

But that proved difficult. It was already after ten o'clock and the main street was dark and quiet. At length, we found a small hotel with inviting lights and asked the woman at the desk if she would place a call to Athens.

"Too late!" she said with a frown. "Tomorrow after eight it will be possible." Apparently her English didn't stretch far enough for an explanation, but her emphatic shake of the head convinced us we would have to wait.

"Well, tomorrow then," said Peter. "But can you tell us where we can eat?"

"There is taverna open, two streets to left," said our frowning friend. "Also big hotel on hill."

So we went to the taverna, a smoky, smelly little place that provided hot, spicy sausages, tomatoes, rolls, and black olives. I was so hungry and so worried about Bart, I hardly cared that the food was not up to all the other wonderful meals we'd had in Greece. I was glad when we left the place.

"Ugh!" I said to Peter.

He gave my hand a comforting squeeze. "We can't expect perfection *every* time, Marty."

We were walking uphill in the shadow of a wall topped with oleander blossoms, neither breaking the soft night-silence around us. At the foot of the outside stairway to our rooms, Peter stopped and turned to me. He was so nice and reassuring! Even this evening with all its upsetting features had had some good moments. Now, if only he would kiss me!

But he only patted my shoulder gently and said, "Sleep well, little Marty." That was all.

I was awake very early the next morning. I stepped onto the little balcony and looked across at the big hotel where we had spent so much of the previous evening. The gardens in front were empty and no cars circled the driveway. They all rested quietly in the car park at the far side. The car park! Wouldn't those men have a car? Surely that's how they would transport Bart. Would they keep him locked in the car? We should have thought of that the night before.

I ducked back into my room and dressed quickly. Blue jeans to blend with all the other young people I had seen climbing on and off buses. I could hear sounds downstairs, so Mrs. Papagoris must be up. After a quick rap on Peter's door, I went down to look for breakfast.

"I go to market," said Mrs. Papagoris in her stilted English. "The coffee and rolls are here. You will help yourself." She smiled. "You were in late last night, yes?"

"Yes," I replied. "We must leave today."

"Leave? You do not wait for Stephanos to return?"

"We'll telephone him this morning. Can you tell me how to find the phone?"

She was describing where the main exchange was located when Peter came into the dining room.

"I've told her we're leaving today," I explained. "We'd better pay her before she goes off to shop."

We settled our bill and ate the breakfast set out for us. After Mrs. Papagoris left, we discussed our plans.

"We'll check bus connections first," said Peter. "By then, Steve should be in his office and we'll put the call through to him."

"But Peter! They must have a car here! We ought to look in the car park at the hotel."

"Let's get started then. Are your bags packed if we have to catch the bus in a hurry?"

"Never unpacked," I said, smiling.

CHAPTER 11

"I'll come!" said Steve when we reached him at his office. "I should be able to get away on Wednesday— that's the day after tomorrow. There's a little hotel called the Argos beyond the square in Kalambaka. Try to stay there. You take a bus to Patras and another to Lamia. At Patras, a ferry crosses the Gulf of Corinth. From there you go north, a long trip but shorter than returning to Athens and traveling with me."

We had already figured that out: six hours back to Athens and another six north to Kalambaka. To go directly from Olympia to Kalambaka would surely take less time than that. I remembered how I had originally thought of Greece as small!

"The police!" I hissed to Peter, who was doing the talking. "Ask him what he thinks about going to the police."

"I heard," said the crisp voice from the telephone. "Wait until I come. Unless you have more definite evidence against the men who are holding Mr. Mickelson, I think it will be better that I am with you. I will see you in the afternoon on Wednesday." He wished us a good journey and hung up.

We found the bus station in a tiny room tacked onto a grocery store. Amid fumes of garlic and spiced meats, a stout woman at a shabby desk seemed to understand only the words "bus" and "ticket." She could not believe we wanted to go in the opposite direction from Athens. When I showed her my map, however, she produced tickets that matched the strange Greek spelling of the towns we would pass through.

Our bus left in two hours, plenty of time to climb the hill to the big hotel again and investigate the cars parked there. We had just reached the circular driveway, however, when we saw a dark gray Mercedes sweep up to the hotel entrance.

Through the windshield, we could see the bald-headed man slouched over the steering wheel. A smaller man beside him popped out and opened the rear door. He was the non-Greek of the group we had seen last night, the one called Thomas.

Down the steps of the hotel came the two others, supporting between them a tall figure in crumpled clothes, brown slacks and a brown tweed jacket.

Though his head hung down and I could not see his face, I was certain it was Bart!

I had started forward, my mouth opened to call out, when Peter fastened my arms in an iron grip. "Not now, Marty! Be quiet! They haven't seen us—don't make them look this way!"

"But I *know* it's Bart! We've got to help him!"

"No! Not now! There's nothing we can do, and it's better if they don't know we're here."

I was sobbing. "But we have to, Peter! Please!" The iron hold kept me rooted to the spot. For a moment I hated him. My white knight had turned rusty.

As the two men half lifted, half dragged the third into the back seat, his loafer fell off. One of the men picked it up and, as he did, something fell out of it. Not noticing, the man tossed the shoe into the car and climbed in himself.

The Mercedes drove smoothly away down the other side of the circle. I turned to Peter angrily, but he had dropped my arm and was pulling a notebook and pencil from his pocket.

"I've got the license number," he said calmly, just as though the whole purpose of our being there wasn't passing out of sight. "Now let's see what dropped out of that shoe."

Just where the loafer had fallen, we found a small piece of paper. It looked crushed and worn. I couldn't believe my eyes as Peter very carefully unfolded it. I recognized my own handwriting!

Peter handed the paper to me and I realized it was the last letter I had sent to Bart. Then, beneath my signature, I saw some fainter writing.

Happy birthday, Marty. Hate missing celebration. In Santa Luzia Hospital, pneumonia. Presents coming. . . . The cable Bart had sent me for my birthday! How strange to see the words as he must have written them in his hospital bed. There was a line crossed out, and then: *Give small one special care. Love you, need you, too. Bart.*

I stared and stared. He hadn't meant to use our special signal after all! He'd intended just to send his love in the same wording I myself had used earlier. Had he changed it later or had some Portuguese—a nurse? an operator?—confused the "too" with "two"? I had no way of knowing, but at least we now had proof we had seen my father.

I cried on Peter's shoulder for a minute and then explained quickly about the letter and the cable. He nodded in sympathy and said gently, "Now I want to see if we can get some names from the hotel."

So in we went. As we approached the large, bustling registration counter, I blew my nose and tried to look as nonchalant as Peter.

"Perhaps you can help us," he said to the brisk young man behind the counter. At least my partner was very much at home in hotels. "The party that just left. I think I recognized them as the men I was supposed to meet here. Can you tell me their names?"

"Ah, the doctor and his party? They go only to take a sick friend to his hotel. You are to meet Dr. Nigrita here?"

"I wish I could wait," said Peter. "Unfortunately, my bus leaves in a few minutes."

"You will perhaps leave a note?"

"Yes—yes, of course." I hoped I was the only one who could tell that he was unprepared for the suggestion.

He took the sheet of paper and envelope from the clerk and moved down the counter, out of the way of a gaily dressed couple who moved up to ask questions in rapid Italian. In a moment, he handed the sealed envelope across the desk and turned away.

We walked silently out of the hotel. As soon as we were on the sunny driveway again, I burst out with questions.

"*What* did you write in the note?"

"Nothing. Just a blank piece of paper. I hope it won't arouse any suspicions from Dr. Nigrita, should he return. We could go to the police now, Marty. We have seen Bart and we know the license number of the car they took him in. We even know the man's name who seems to be in charge. And there's the letter."

But time was running out. We had less than half

an hour until our bus left and, for all we knew, Dr. Nigrita's car was already on its way to Kalambaka. We did not believe for a minute that they were taking Bart to another hotel. It seemed terribly important, therefore, that we not delay our departure until the next day's bus.

We discussed our predicament as we went quickly down the hill. If the police believed us, we would have to stay in Olympia while they looked for the Mercedes. If they did not believe the damning facts we had or if they did not find Dr. Nigrita, we would have missed the bus and would have to wait another day to go to Kalambaka. In the meantime, we might lose all chance of catching up with Bart again.

It was a no-win situation. On the one hand, we were certain they had my father with them and we knew where they were going. On the other, if we tried to get help in Olympia, we might arrive in Kalambaka too late to do him any good. And Steve would be meeting us in Kalambaka, where he could be much more convincing with the police. With many misgivings, my decision was to take the bus.

Somewhat out of breath, we were standing in front of the bus station with our suitcases when that battered, dusty vehicle pulled up. Men, women, and children climbed off and luggage, piled high on the roof, was tossed to the ground. Hikers collected backpacks and two giggling girls walked away carrying a crate of cackling chickens between them. The driver crossed the street to a taverna and the bus was empty. No one showed any interest in getting *on*.

Peter and I stood in the hot sun, the perspiration trickling down our foreheads. Ten minutes passed. Fifteen. Then the bus driver strolled back across the street. He hoisted our bags to the roof and collected our tickets. We mounted the steps and took seats near the front. Others came straggling back and, within a few minutes, the bus was full again.

It felt good to sit down. When the bus finally started, a strong breeze whipped through the open windows, cooling us quickly. We rolled westward along a good road to Pyrgos, a little town that housed the overflow of tourists visiting ancient Olympia. Our stop there was brief and added only a few passengers to our load.

From Pyrgos, we wound north along the western coast of the Peloponnese, sometimes seeing the blue water of the Ionic Sea but, more often, only rough and treeless hills. Close to the sea were little homesteads surrounded by expanses of truck gardens. Sturdy figures hoed long rows of vegetables and, occasionally, plastic-covered greenhouses rose in clusters like diminutive Quonset huts.

Wherever there were houses, there were flowers: climbing roses, nasturtiums, and oleanders. The scenery kept me absorbed until we reached the city of Patras and disembarked for lunch.

We had a different bus and a new driver as we crept along in a double line of cars waiting to board the ferry.

"Watch for that Mercedes," Peter warned me. "They either have to come this way or cross the bridge at Corinth, and we know this way is more direct."

"But they may take the other man back to Athens. You know they said only three would go to Kalambaka."

"True," said Peter. "But he could go by bus."

We moved forward slowly and bumped up the ramp onto the ferry. Our driver wedged us into a slot between a high-sided truck and a row of passenger cars. The door of the bus opened but only two or three people rose to get off.

Peter said, "You can stay here if you want to but I'm going to take a look around."

I didn't want to stay on the hot bus but I didn't feel like squeezing through the cars packed around us either. As I watched Peter's departing back, I curled up uncomfortably in my hard seat and wondered if we were doing the right thing.

I still couldn't believe I had actually been close to Bart and had not even let him know I was there. Common sense told me he was drugged and wouldn't have known even if I had called, but somehow I felt I should have. I grudgingly agreed it was better that Dr. Nigrita and his friends not be aware we were on their trail, but I still had a sense of failure: we had found Bart and now we had lost him again.

I pushed to the bottom of my shoulder bag and fingered the little icon. Its presence seemed a talisman pointing to Kalambaka, the place those awful men planned to do away with Bart. I shuddered in the stifling heat and watched for Peter.

He came back a little later, shaking his head. "No Mercedes on board. I looked at all the cars and went up to the bow of the ferry where all the people are. We're almost across; the gulf's not very wide here.

There was a bump and a grinding of boat and pilings. Our driver swung into his seat and started the engine. Slowly, the neighboring truck edged forward and the bus, with many jerks, followed it onto the mainland of Greece.

To our right rose the walls of an old fortress. I saw a few tired-looking buildings and then we were on a wide road heading east along the edge of the gulf.

My head nodded and I slept against Peter's shoulder, his arm bracing me against the jiggle of the ride. It seemed only a minute until he shook me gently.

"Marty, you must see this! We are almost to Itea and the bay is so blue!"

I opened my eyes to a harbor of ships, freighters, and fishing boats, spattered across water of the same bright shade in which seas are printed on four-color maps. Mountains, the highest we'd seen, rose mistily beyond the little town of Itea.

The bus paused for an exchange of passengers and some clambering about on its roof to retrieve luggage. Then we were off again, leaving the water and climbing a twisting highway where every turn brought a fresh vista of the harbor below.

"Did you know these are olive trees?" asked Peter presently. I had imagined olives would grow like peaches in an orchard, not in vast forests of twisted trunks and soft gray-green leaves, but we were surrounded by gnarled old trees lifting their branches high above the top of the bus. I remembered Vicki's telling us how they were passed down from generation to generation and that often the ownership of a single tree went with a bride as a dowry gift.

Another road joined ours from the east and a sign clearly read DELPHI 10 KM. I sighed: a dream, so close yet having no part in our present mission.

In the next village, Amfissa, we climbed off the bus with the others and shared grapefruit juice in the shade of an olive tree. It was already after three o'clock and we were not yet at Lamia. I studied my map and decided we were only halfway to Kalambaka: it would be dark before we reached the end of our journey.

In another hour and a half, we pulled up by a pretty, shaded square in Lamia and persuaded the bus driver

105

we needed our bags from the roof of the bus. The bus station was hot and smelly, but the smiling agent showed us where to leave our things, examined our tickets, and drew a large *1830* on a slip of paper. We would leave for Kalambaka at six-thirty.

There was plenty of time to eat, and we chose a scrubbed iron table under the trees in the park-like square. Bread, cheese, and soup tasted like the most elegant of dishes, but I had to force down the tiny cup of thick black coffee as if it were a dose of medicine.

The bells in a nearby church were tolling for six o'clock when Peter grabbed my arm. I looked where he pointed and there, rounding the square, was a dark gray Mercedes.

"There're three men in it! That's all I can see," he exclaimed. He left the table quickly and covered the distance to the far corner in long strides. The car was pinned in a slow-moving line of traffic and crept past two sides of the square. Just as it started up the third, it made a sweeping turn onto a street angling off to the west.

Peter strode back. "It's them all right! I got a good look at the license plate when they made the turn. And that's the road to Trikala—the one we'll take. They must have dropped the other man just as we thought."

"Didn't you see Bart?"

"No, but he could have been lying on the back seat."

"Let's go find our bus," I said, standing up. "At least we know we're headed in the right direction."

Peter looked at me questioningly. "No more tears, Marty? We're doing our best, you know. And I don't think they have any idea we're looking for Bart."

"No more tears. I'm sorry, Peter. You've been such a help and I don't know what I'd do without you. Now, where's that bus?"

CHAPTER 12

The bus arrived late. It had come from Athens and was already crammed with people.

We found seats in the back, but not together. The woman I sat beside held a wiggling child and spoke Greek in a friendly tone of voice. I could only smile and dart longing glances at the bits of scenery that showed beyond the bobbing head of the child.

It was a long ride to Trikala, nearly sixty miles. The dusk was already turning into night when we stopped and my seat companions got off. Peter promptly slipped into the spot beside me and, in a little while, we started on the last leg of the endless trip.

About nine o'clock, we rumbled down into the center of Kalambaka. The bus pulled up where the main street widened into a cobbled, hollow square. We collected our suitcases and followed the street as it passed beyond the square. Sure enough, a small sign above a shadowy entrance in a blank, plastered wall announced ARGOS HOTEL.

The room inside was shadowy, too, but a pool of light surrounded the reception desk. A stooped old man appeared from the gloom and made a stiff little bow.

"Good evening," said Peter. "Do you speak English?"

"Good evening, sir and madam," the man responded in a rusty voice. "I speak a little."

"Do you have two rooms available?"

"I do. Rooms at the back where you will see the morning sun upon the rocks of the gods. Will you register then?" With shaky hands, he fumbled in a drawer and laid two cards on the desk.

"Do you know Stephanos Nakrodis in Athens?" I asked as I filled out my card.

"Stephanos? Him I have not seen of late, but his mother's people live in this valley."

"He told us about your hotel. He's going to meet us here day after tomorrow."

"He will be welcome." Two keys rattled as he took them from their hooks. "Your rooms are at the top of the stairs and to the left. I regret we no longer serve meals since my daughters have gone to Athens. It is only my grandson and myself who keep the hotel."

We climbed creaky stairs while I speculated on what

the rooms in this spooky place would be like. Several closed doors lined the dimly lit hallway but, as the man had promised, two on our left stood open. Peter fumbled for the light switch in the first, and a bare bulb glared from the center of the ceiling.

The room was neat, though a little shabby. A bed, a straight chair, and a table were along one wall. Facing them was a large wardrobe cabinet in place of a closet. Heavy draperies were looped back from a tall window. Peering out, I could see the outline of a shallow balcony. The lighting here was either feast or famine: a tiny lamp on the table gave only a sickly glow through its pink ruffled shade.

Peter's room was like mine, and we found a large, quaint bathroom across the hall.

"Good night, Marty," said Peter, patting my shoulder in his usual brotherly manner.

"Good night, Peter," I whispered and hopefully lifted my face toward his. A quick peck of a kiss landed on my nose and he was gone, his door closing softly.

So much for those mutual responses you read about! I should have been concentrating on Bart, anyhow. I was, really, but not for long because I was asleep almost before I stretched out on the bed's hard mattress.

The rocks of the gods! My first view of the towering Meteora next morning was all that the old man had promised. Rising beyond the dark buildings outside my window, jagged spikes of sheer rock fenced the horizon. The first rays of the sun were creaming the very tips of the columns like spotlights on castle turrets.

My window slid reluctantly to its widest opening and I stepped out onto the balcony. I could get a broader view now of the phenomenon of the Meteora. Each towering crag was separated from its neighbor, yet so close together were they that they seemed an inpenetrable forest of steely gray.

Vicki had described how hermits found refuge on their tops hundreds of years ago, followed by the persecuted Christians who arrived in the twelfth and thirteenth centuries. They had started building monasteries in the 1300's, perching one on each rocky summit until there were twenty-four in all, sanctuaries that flourished for nearly three hundred years.

My imagination stretched to encompass the remoteness of a life spent on top of one of those pinnacles. Now the sun's rays struck them more strongly, turning them a glowing golden red like the fiery teeth of a giant comb still swathed in darkness.

I tiptoed to Peter's window and tapped. A tousled head emerged from a bump of covers on the bed, and a hand waved languidly. The window was open two inches at the bottom and I hissed through the space.

"You're missing a terrific sunrise—wait 'til you see it!" I ducked back into my own room to dress, jeans

111

again, and a long-sleeved shirt. Vicki had warned that women were only admitted to the monasteries if their flesh was covered.

Twenty minutes later, we laid our keys on the reception desk and slipped out of the sleeping hotel to hunt some breakfast. The street still lay in shadow but the upper half of the square was already lighted by the sun. A lovely aroma of fresh-baked bread was in the air and we traced it to a little bakery close to where the bus had stopped the night before.

Inside, small tables squatted along a padded bench like cocktail tables in the club car of a train. We pointed to rolls and honey-covered buns in the gleaming glass showcase, and a teenage boy brought them to our table.

Our sign language made him chuckle. "Café, yes?" he asked and produced two large cups of steaming coffee.

"Where shall we start?" I buttered the last of my honey bun. "We passed a couple of hotels last night where Dr. Nigrita could be staying, but Mrs. Nakrodis thought my icon came from the monasteries up on the rocks. Could they be keeping Bart in one of them?"

There would be dozens of ravines among those tall stony spires, too. I didn't want Peter to know how much the thought of them weighed on my mind. Please, God, let us find Bart before he landed in a ravine!

"We've got a whole day to scout around," Peter

said. "Steve won't be here until tomorrow afternoon, so I vote for going up to the monasteries first and checking out the icon. According to Vicki, there're only four or five we can get into."

It wasn't just the little icon that called us to go up to the Meteora, or even the possibility that Bart was somewhere among them; anyone who saw those majestic spires would be drawn to scale their heights.

"How do we get there? It looks like a long walk."

"There ought to be a bus," said Peter. "Let's look around."

We paid our bill and went out into the square. A shiny tour bus zoomed past, headed up the valley, a couple of small cars following in its wake. Groups of children carrying school books scurried noisily down the cross street. Women in black dresses and scuffed sandals lugged bags bulging with long loaves of bread.

A stubby vehicle like a mini school bus stood in the square. Several of the somber women were climbing aboard, and Peter approached the driver.

"You go to Meteora?"

A stream of Greek flowed over us. Somehow Peter found a clue. "It goes as far as Kastraki," he said. "That's the village at the foot of the rocks, I think. Let's go that far, anyhow."

We joined the chattering women and jounced slowly out of Kalambaka, the rocks rising abruptly from the sloping fields on our right. As the town dropped behind, I saw a high, misty range of mountains poised beyond the wide valley to our left.

A dozen goats were scattered on the road bank, a bent old man in flowing robes standing guard. In the distance, other shepherds roamed among their flocks. There was a vastness about the scene: the broad valley, the sheer cliffs at the base of the Meteora rocks, the faraway mountains, and the white gravel of the river's flood plain below the climbing road.

The bus stopped often to discharge the women and their bags of food. The sixth jerking halt was in a little village, a tumbled collection of houses where the road turned steeply toward a gap in the wall of rocks. The remaining passengers filed off, Peter and I at the rear. This was Kastraki, dwarfed by the first stony spires that began only a little farther on.

We walked up the street among houses sprinkled across the hillside like a handful of popcorn tossed from the rocks above. At the upper edge of the village we saw that it was still a long way to the top of the gap.

A dusty van stopped beside us and a bearded face looked out the window.

"Ride, friend?" asked an American voice. "We're going to the top. Lots of room!"

"Great!" I exclaimed. "Come on, Peter, this is just what we need."

We squatted on a pile of sleeping bags behind the

driver and a skinny girl with sleepy eyes. "You American, too?" asked our driver. "I'm from Chicago. Just came from Delphi—now there's a terrific place." The van rounded a curve and passed between two needle-like pinnacles. From the back, we could see little else except the high road banks.

"We're going to St. Stephan's first," he rattled on. "They say the view is terrific and I want this morning light to get some pictures. Got a telephoto lens like you wouldn't believe."

The girl murmured, "*Agios Stephanos*."

"She's Greek," he explained. "We met in Athens— I stayed in the Plaka awhile 'til she said I ought to see the countryside." We chugged up and around more curves. "Well, here we are! If you're ready to leave when we are, I'll take you down again."

"Thanks very much," said Peter. I could tell he disapproved of their casual ménage. "We'll be up here most of the day, I think."

"Good luck with your pictures!" I called as we left them sorting camera equipment.

The van had stopped in a parking area beyond which a sturdy wooden footbridge led across a rocky crevass. The solid gray walls of the Monastery of St. Stephan rose from the very brink of the ravine. A small arched doorway, like a rathole in a wainscoting, was the only opening in the massive walls.

The doorway led to a dark and clammy passage and

then to stone steps. At the top, a sunny courtyard was enclosed by other stone buildings, tubs of flowers dispelling the severity of their walls. A black-robed nun at a little table asked for a few drachmas and waved us on past whitewashed arches.

Suddenly the buildings were behind us and the whole valley of the Pinios lay spread below. Only a knee-high balustrade of stone marked the edge of a straight drop of hundreds of feet to the sloping fields. The miniature rooftops of Kalambaka lay at our feet.

Beyond the town, empty fields stretched to the chalky whiteness of the river's flood plain. The Pinios itself was a trickle of oil leaking through the sun-bleached gravel. On the other side of the valley, many miles away, rose the high, rugged mountains like a painted backdrop for a Western movie.

The effect overwhelmed me: in a vast, majestic world such as this, how could we, two tiny ants, find another tiny ant named Bart? But against the stark beauty of the immense landscape, it was no wonder the monks and hermits of old had come here to find peace and tranquility for their meditations.

Peter's arm slipped around my shoulders as we looked and looked. "I'll always remember this—and you," he said in such a low voice that I barely made out the words. I held my breath to hear more.

"A great spot!" Our Chicago friend bounded to our sides with his camera, and the spell was broken.

Reluctantly we turned away and retraced our steps to the courtyard. Arched columns of a narrow porch drew us to the nuns' chapel. We entered a small bare room whose only ornaments were a few pictures hung in the traditional pattern along the whitewashed walls, the colors of the portraits surprisingly bright.

A handful of tourists moved aside and I saw a familiar pose: a hooded Virgin with head bent to the cheek of the little Child. My own icon was out of my bag in a flash and I compared the two pictures, the expressions, the position of the hands, the folds of clothing. The match was almost exact.

"Peter!" I whispered. "This is it! This is where my icon came from!"

CHAPTER 13

Peter took the little icon and studied it gravely. I looked at the other pictures on the walls but there were none like the old man with the white beard.

"We'll ask that nun," he said, indicating the silent woman fussing with a row of votive candles.

She looked at the icon, nodded, and addressed us in Greek. When she saw our blank faces, she led us out of the chapel and across the courtyard to a little room that served as a gift shop. A dozen tourists filled the space between the door and the counter but our guide slid neatly through the crowd.

In a moment, a sweet-faced sister leaned toward us across the counter. "You have an icon you wish to match? May I see?"

She examined both pictures and turned to another nun who was making change. We were jostled aside by a large woman with flaming red hair.

As the crowd thinned, we moved close to the counter again. Rows of small icons were spread out for display, single paintings and double ones like mine. Their sizes ranged from two inches high to five or six. The pictures portrayed several different religious figures, but most were poor attempts and the wooden slabs on which they were mounted did not show the delicate carving that was on mine.

"This is a beautiful piece," said the second nun, handing it back to me. "We have none like it. Indeed, St. Nikolas does not appear in any of our paintings. The house dedicated to him is no longer occupied, but the order that dwells in the Varlaam has care of the relics. This likeness is unmistakable." She smiled wistfully. "The Virgin is a beautiful copy from our sanctuary. Before the Germans came, we had many treasures such as that."

"The Germans?" I asked.

"Yes, during the war, they were located here in this spot. Such destruction they left, those Nazis! It was only afterward that my order was permitted to come and attempt to reconstruct."

"Thank you very, very much for your help," I said. "I really need to find out all I can about this icon."

"There is a book. Perhaps you would like to see the pictures of the other sanctuaries?"

From my dwindling supply of drachmas, I bought a thick paper-backed booklet of colored photographs.

Peter and I sat on a bench in the sunny courtyard and looked at the pictures, reading the few words of stilted English that described them. Toward the back was St. Nikolas, complete with bald head, white beard, and robe covered with black crosses. He too carried a large red book, just as in the painting on my icon.

A shadow fell across the page as a man sat down beside me.

"That is a beautiful icon you hold," he said in the clipped tones of an Englishman. "May I be so forward as to ask where you obtained it?"

The abrupt approach startled me and I glanced at Peter. His face was impassive but his eyes signaled alarm. Only then did I turn to face the stranger.

"It was . . . " My voice trailed off. I was looking into the eyes of the sandy-haired man with the wire-rimmed glasses, the man called Thomas whom I had last seen getting into a gray Mercedes in front of the hotel in Olympia. ". . . a gift," I finished firmly, hoping my surprise had not been too evident.

"A gift from—?" began the man.

"Excuse us, please," said Peter, getting to his feet and pulling me roughly away from the bench. "Our ride is waiting for us."

"One moment!" exclaimed the man. But we had joined a crowd of tourists flowing toward the passage and the parking lot. In the dark of the tunnel, we slipped ahead as quickly as possible and were just behind the guide as we crossed the wooden bridge. A large bus waited at the other end.

"Get on as if we belong with the tour," Peter muttered in my ear. "They won't notice two extra right away."

We climbed into the rear door and slipped onto the seat across the back. The others piled in and the doors closed. The guide walked along the aisle, counting heads. She was halfway to the back when she looked up and I saw it was Vicki Nakrodis.

"There are too many!" she exclaimed as she reached the back of the bus. Then she looked at our faces. "Peter and Marty! But how do you get here? You are not on my tour."

"Oh, Vicki, are we ever glad to see you! Please let us ride to the next monastery—we have to get away from this place quickly," I pleaded.

"Here he comes," said Peter, looking out the big tinted window. "We would really appreciate a lift to your next stop, Vicki. Could we pay, or something?"

"No, no, I really should put you off. It's against the rules. But I won't do that." She called to the bus driver in Greek and he gunned his motor as he pulled away from the parked cars. She dropped onto the seat beside us. "Now tell me what you are doing stowed away on my tour."

I sneaked a look out the back window and saw the sandy-haired man shuffling among the cars, peering into each one.

"We found out something about Marty's icon," Peter explained, "and while we were sitting in the courtyard, a man came along and started asking questions. He's in the gang that has Marty's father. We followed them from Olympia to Kalambaka yesterday."

Vicki looked startled. "*You* followed them? But how—but now I see why Stephanos comes here tomorrow. He had only said he was coming for a few days to take more photographs."

"Yes, we're meeting him tomorrow. Today we are trying to find out what the icon means and why Bart sent it to Marty."

"We stop next at Varlaam," Vicki said. "There is a museum there that may be helpful, and you may join my group and learn of the monastery's history. But after that, we travel back to Trikala and on to Volos."

"We'd love to go around Varlaam with you," I said. "I hope you won't get in trouble because we stowed away, but it was so lucky for us that we found you!"

"No, not for this short way." Above her warm smile, her dark eyes were troubled. "I regret that I must go on so soon. You will be all right until Stephanos comes?"

"Of course," Peter assured her. "But you've been a real port in the sea."

"Storm," I murmured as the bus stopped and everyone filed off.

Vicki organized her group at the foot of narrow concrete steps that wound up among the tangled rocks in front of us. No monastery was in sight, only the steep sides of another gray-scarred pinnacle.

"We'll try to stay in the middle of the group until we see if any more of Dr. Nigrita's friends are around," whispered Peter. "If we're lucky, Thomas hasn't figured out where we went."

So we toured another, more elaborate monastery and listened to Vicki's familiar voice. She related the story of the early monks and how rope ladders and baskets, let down by pulleys, had long been the only way to reach this high place.

In the dimly lit museum, we discovered several pictures of St. Nikolas, *Agios Nicolaos,* as the Greeks called him. One was a single icon not much larger than the one I carried. Under the dusty glass case, it looked identical. Vicki questioned a slim young monk who was arranging books on the shelves that covered one wall. I had the impression he was startled to hear of the icon's twin, but he appeared to answer her politely. He crossed the room with her and held out his hand.

"He wants to examine it," said Vicki. "I'm not sure

what he has in mind. I don't think I would give it to him."

I extended the icon, opened so that both paintings showed, but my fingers were firmly clamped to the sides. His round black monk's hat bent over it and his voice exclaimed in rapid Greek.

"He says it resembles the iconic art of the sixteen hundreds," Vicki translated. "He is anxious to show it to his high priest. He thinks it is of great value and may be one that is missing from their collection."

She listened to more of the flowing Greek. "If you are in a hurry, I would take the icon and go," she whispered. "He doubts it is only a reproduction. But if you wait for him to call the priest, you may be here for several hours."

It was thrilling to think my icon might belong here, but I couldn't part with it until I discovered what Bart had meant by sending it to me. Moreover, Peter and I didn't dare become involved until we found my father. Even if I was rude, I had to break away.

Pulling the icon from the young monk's gentle touch, I said loudly, "Well, thank you very much." I stuffed it into my shoulder bag and hurried toward the door, leaving Peter to say our goodbyes to Vicki.

In a few moments, he joined me in the bright sunlight and we began the long descent to the road.

"Whew!" I exploded. "That icon really makes things

happen around here. What do you think it all means?"

"I'm wondering if there's a scheme to steal icons from these monasteries," said Peter thoughtfully. "They would bring a lot of money on the black market."

"And Bart might have found out about it! If it's illegal and someone in the bank is involved, he would really be upset."

"The thieves could even be smuggling them out of the country," Peter suggested eagerly. "That might explain the 'trail' he was following in Lisbon."

"And if he knew my icon is one of the missing ones, perhaps sending it to me was his way of keeping it safe. I must have a valuable piece of evidence right here in my bag."

"Hold it!" Peter whispered and grabbed my arm. We had just crossed an iron bridge over a deep ravine between the rocks, and he was leading the way around the last jutting cornice before the final steps to the roadway. "That man is just starting up from the bottom—the one that talked to you at St. Stephan's."

He pulled me off the walk and onto a faint path circling behind the cornice and along the edge of the ravine. We slipped and slithered as we climbed down among the loose stones.

A final slide and we were on the road well below the parking area and out of sight of the steps. A hundred yards away, on the other side, was the entrance to still another monastery, with a small sign in English saying RESTAURANT.

"Let's take time out to eat," I said. "My thoughts are all mixed up."

"I hope Thomas isn't hungry, too," Peter added grimly, but he didn't hesitate to climb the twisting steps set into the rocks. Happily, a good many other sightseers had the same idea, and we moved slowly up with the crowd.

This was the monastery of the Transfiguration of Christ, the largest group of buildings we had seen. Here on the rock's top was ample room for a dozen rusty tables along an open porch. Black-garbed monks stood out sharply among the brighter holiday clothes of their visitors as they brought bowls of thick soup and chunks of black bread. Peter and I found a table by the inner wall where we could keep careful watch over the people coming and going. It was a peaceful spot, and no one paid us any attention.

"I've seen enough monasteries for awhile," I said between spoonfuls of soup. "If we go back to Kalambaka now, we might be able to find the hotel where Dr. Nigrita is staying. It would help to know that before Steve gets here tomorrow."

Peter nodded. "We can hike back to that last little village and take the bus. At least the road to Kastraki is all downhill."

We finished our meal and, without even entering the monastery, descended to the road again. There were fewer people about, and we saw no one we recognized.

The walk took an hour. Cars and buses passed occasionally, some going our way and some headed for the monasteries above, but none stopped. The first half-mile was through deep shadow, the gigantic rocks shutting out the sunlight and their sheer, gray bases rising close on either side. Presently, however, the rocks pulled back and the road wound down through stony pastureland. A shepherd's dog deserted his flock of goats and came to bark ferociously at us.

The first houses of Kastraki appeared, bare and worn as though all color and vegetation had been blown away by the wind. They stood well away from the main road, clustered along paths of packed dirt. As the houses grew thicker, some of the paths widened into lanes. Just beyond one of these, Peter stopped.

"Marty!" he exclaimed in a low voice. "I saw the rear of a gray car up that lane. If it's a Mercedes, that's just one coincidence too many."

"You think it's Dr. Nigrita's car?"

"It could be. Let's go back up the road and follow the path just above this one. We can get a good look from there without anybody seeing us."

We retraced our steps to a weedy path that threaded its way between small stone stables and shabby houses squatting under low roofs of broken tile.

A few chickens scratched in the dooryards and a baby cried from a decrepit baby buggy. An old crone in black shuffled past carrying a bucket of water, her eyes glued to the ground. It was a bleak place, this corner of Kastraki tucked under the towering Meteora.

We were in shadow again as we neared the end of the pathetic row of buildings. There were no people, dogs, or chickens when we turned off the path and crept along the side of a crumbling shed. As we peered around its corner, I could see we were directly over the lane below and slightly beyond its last house. Beside that final cottage stood the sleek Mercedes.

CHAPTER 14

Like the others we had passed, the cottage below was one story, and it too had a tiled roof with broken edges. The wall facing us was pierced by a single window, a black square without glass or curtain. It was tucked high under the overhanging tiles as though seeking protection from the chilly winds that blew from the rocks above.

Except for the swish of an occasional car on the road to the monasteries, the air was still. The high voices of women arguing several lanes away drifted up to us, the tap of someone's hammer punctuating their Greek chatter. We were in an unreal world: very old, slightly smelly, and oddly peaceful in the afternoon sun.

Sounds from the house below us came as a surprise, breaking the spell of this desolate spot. A door slammed and gruff voices grew louder.

Two men appeared beside the Mercedes and I recognized Dr. Nigrita at once. The other was the tall, bald man. They were apparently speaking to someone still out of sight.

Peter's fingers dug into my shoulder, pushing me behind the shed's broken wall. He crouched beside me and looked cautiously over the heaped stones. I heard car doors close and the powerful motor erupt.

"The car's leaving," Peter whispered. "But someone's staying at the house. Maybe more than one—I can't tell."

Without moving from my protected corner, I could see the Mercedes as it eased along the lane and out onto the main road. It turned uphill toward the monasteries.

"Off to collect Thomas, I expect," said Peter. "They may be back."

"We'd better wait," I said. "One of us should stay here and the other watch the road in case the car goes straight down and back to Kalambaka."

"I'll scout the road," Peter volunteered. "It's easier for a man to wander around in a place like this. Less questions asked."

I didn't argue. I wanted to keep the little stone cottage in sight. It seemed just the sort of place these awful men would keep a prisoner, and perhaps my father was there.

As Peter slipped away to the upper path and out

to the road, I settled more or less comfortably against my stony backrest. I could see over the tumbledown wall but I was well screened by the high, coarse grass that grew down the slope to the back of the cottage. How far was it? Farther than the length of a swimming pool, surely, but not so far as two lengths. Ninety feet popped into my mind, but I've never been good at judging distance.

For awhile, the scene was very peaceful. A scrawny brown dog came with a wagging tail, sniffed my shoes, and skittered on his way. A half-dozen crowlike birds settled in the branches of a twisted olive tree off to the left and argued about their next meal. The growl of a bus and the shrill voices of children announced that the school day was over.

Then a big, tough-looking man appeared around the corner of the house. He wore baggy black pants and a coarse blue shirt open at the neck. Even from the distance, he looked like a mean character with his thick neck, beady eyes, and swooping black mustache.

He came directly to the rear of the cottage and turned his back. It took me a moment to understand his errand but, after a long interval, he turned again and strolled back the way he had come.

As he rounded the corner, I heard him speaking to someone. There were at least two men on guard, then. Somehow I was sure they *were* "on guard" and that the object they guarded was Bart.

The shadows from the Meteora rocks grew deeper and stretched over and beyond the village. Odors of garlic and frying food floated past me; already it was the supper hour. I was beginning to worry about Peter when I heard stealthy steps behind me. He dropped wearily down onto the bumpy ground.

"I've made the rounds," he said. "The Mercedes went past, straight down the hill, about an hour ago, with three men inside. Then I went down a couple of lanes and got a look at the house from the front."

"Did you see anyone? There're at least two men— I've heard them talking."

"There's a bench and table outside, and two men were sitting and smoking when I first saw them. Then one ducked around to the back and I was afraid he might have seen you."

"Call of nature," I explained.

"So now they're fixing their supper. Shall we head back to town?"

"I want to look in that window," I said. "If they're eating, maybe we could sneak down."

"Seems kind of risky. It would be safer to wait until dark."

"Ugh!" I groaned. "Other people get hungry, too."

"There's a funny little shop just down the hill," said Peter. "I'll go get some bread and cheese. Maybe I can find out how late the buses run. Kalambaka would be a long walk in the dark."

"Get some juice, too, please. I'm terribly thirsty. And be careful." I squeezed his hand as he got to his feet. He gave my head a little pat before he slipped away into the shadows.

I thought about Bart. The feeling that he was as close as the cottage just down the hill was very strong. I considered playing a lost tourist and approaching the men who sat at the front. But I couldn't question them in Greek and I was sure they would never let me go inside the house. The only way was to look into that high little window, and Peter was right about its needing to be night to do that.

Peter came back very soon, bringing a big wedge of cheese wrapped in greasy paper, a long loaf of bread not wrapped at all, and a medium-sized can of grape-fruit juice.

"Bad news," he said as he used the opener on his penknife to punch holes in the can. "The last local bus was just pulling out when I got to the store. No more until six tomorrow morning."

"So we walk," I said philosophically, munching on bread and cheese. "Everything's quiet at the cottage, and it's getting dark pretty fast."

Peter slurped juice from the can and handed it to me. "I never liked grapefruit juice before I came to Greece," he commented. "But I never liked American girls with green eyes before, either."

I almost choked on my cheese. It was the first real

compliment he'd ever paid me. I was trying to swallow the cheese so I could tell him what *I* thought about tall, wiry Swiss men when a little light flickered in the dark hole of the window below us.

"Someone's in there with a lighted match," Peter whispered.

"Maybe they're feeding him," I murmured. The light flickered out.

We sat very still, staring at the black opening. Nothing happened for a long time. Then the deep shadows at the side of the cottage seemed to move and break up as a feeble light appeared. A faint, glowing dot bobbled around the corner of the house like some one-eyed monster.

"Lantern, shuttered," whispered Peter. In a moment I could distinguish three figures shuffling along close together. They stopped at about the same spot where the lone man had earlier, and the glow suddenly blossomed. I saw only one thing in the burst of light— my father's haggard face.

I felt no shock, I had been so sure in my own mind he was here. The light was quickly covered again; perhaps Bart's captors had been untying his hands.

"There's a gag over his mouth," Peter breathed in my ear. "I think he's pretty much doped up, too."

There was nothing we could do. I felt so helpless I could have cried.

134

The shadowy figures merged with the building and disappeared. I kept staring at the place they had been, too numb with relief that Bart was alive and dread for what might happen to him next to think straight.

Peter pulled me to my feet. "We'd better head for Kalambaka," he urged. "We can't tackle those two watchdogs ourselves, but maybe we can get help."

We slipped away from our lookout post and along the path to the road. The village had closed up for the night, the only sounds of life coming from a scattering of lighted windows well away from the highway. In a few minutes, we left even those behind and were on the open road.

For the first ten minutes, we were silent. I was thinking up wild plans for getting Bart out through that little high window and away from his captors. We'd need a flashlight and probably a rope. That might not be hard, but we also needed a car to get him away quickly. I supposed it would be possible to rent one in Kalambaka, but I had only two travelers' checks left and I knew Peter's money was low, too. Besides, the area didn't seem to do much business late in the evening.

Lights of a car appeared far down the road. "Let's duck!" said Peter. "It could be Dr. Nigrita and his friends coming back."

So we made our first detour into the stiff bushes

along the roadside. As the glare of the lights passed, even I could tell the car was small and rattling, with no resemblance to a Mercedes.

Three more times we took to the ditch, but each was a false alarm. As the road swung away from the towering Meteora rocks, the sky became a little lighter. The thin crescent of a moon appeared above the jagged teeth on our left, turning us into small mice scurrying along an impenetrable wall.

I began to have trouble keeping up with Peter's long strides. "Please slow down," I begged. "I don't want you to have to carry me the last ten miles."

He took my hand, his as warm and comforting as ever, and pulled me along.

"I love your sense of humor, Marty." From the tone of his voice, I could tell he was serious. "Will we ever have a chance to sit still and talk—about you and me?"

"Of course we will, Peter!" It was just as well he couldn't see my eyes. They would have said too many things, and I wasn't really sure what he wanted to hear. He was a young man full of ambition and I did not believe he wanted to become involved with an American girl. Romantically, that is, for he was certainly involved wholeheartedly in the search for my father.

The lights of Kalambaka glowed in the distance, another mile, perhaps. I squeezed Peter's hand. "You've been so great to travel around Greece with me. Anybody else would have given up long ago."

"Best vacation I've ever had." He was laughing gently. "I wouldn't have missed it for anything. Except we always seem to be in such a hurry."

Presently we were among small, dark houses and trudging down the long main street of the town. An occasional feeble street light was as welcome as the brightest glare of a big city. There were a few other people strolling, too, and we felt less conspicuous as we neared our hotel.

Peter looked at his watch. "An hour and fifteen minutes. Not good, but then we had those rests in the ditch."

In front of the Argos was a shabby van. "Looks like Steve's," I said. "But he couldn't be here yet."

Peter tried to open the door of the Argos. It was locked. He banged impatiently and someone called from inside. There was the rattle of a bolt, and the door swung open.

CHAPTER 15

"Welcome back!" exclaimed Steve, grabbing us both in an exuberant bear hug. "I was afraid they had caught you, too!"

"How in the world did you get here so soon?" I was breathless from being crushed between my two favorite men. Next to Bart, of course. "We thought you weren't coming until tomorrow."

"Vicki called me at the office just at lunchtime. She told a weird tale about your seeing one of the men you think have your father. It sounded as though you needed help right away, so I cleared my desk and came. But when you weren't here and had not been back all day, I was worried. Tell me about it!"

"Could we go some place and *eat*?" I asked. "Is it too late?"

"I know just the place," said Steve. So, after a quick

trip upstairs to tidy up a bit, I was escorted by my two stalwart friends to a small taverna hidden behind the town square.

We ate something best described as sausage and pancakes. Steve made sure they brought us big cups of "morning coffee" instead of the tiny Turkish ones usually served in the evening. I relaxed a little, but my thoughts remained with Bart.

There were many things to tell Steve. I showed him the paper from Bart's shoe, and Peter told him about the letters scrawled on the stones in the Olympic athletes' tunnel. Added to the conversation we'd overheard on the hotel terrace, today's events convinced him we had stumbled on something even more complex than kidnapping. He wasn't surprised that the paintings on my icon were those of the Meteora monasteries, but he exclaimed excitedly when we told of the young monk's concern in the museum at Varlaam.

In the end, we described the watch we'd kept behind the cottage on the edge of Kastraki and how we had seen Bart dragged out by his guards. I drew a diagram of the location of the cottage and the way the paths and lanes were laid out.

"We should make our move tonight," said Steve, when we had gone over everything we could think of. "Tomorrow night may be too late. The family of the wife of my mother's cousin live in Kastraki, and I believe I know how they could help."

I gulped the rest of my coffee as Steve settled the bill with the taverna's proprietor. "Meet you at the van," he said. "I think I should have a talk with the police before we go."

Twenty minutes later we were driving back up the road to Kastraki. "Will the police come?" I asked.

"Not until morning," said Steve. "The man on duty was not much impressed with my account of the situation. If you were in his place, would you wake your superior because someone told a story of two visitors to Greece who had followed a carful of businessmen from Olympia to Kastraki, and claimed to have recognized a sick man in a house there?"

"Well, the 'sick' man was tied up, and we *did* overhear Dr. Nigrita talk about getting rid of him in a ravine at Meteora," I protested.

"I'm sorry, Marty. I tried, but I do not think I convinced him of the urgency you and Peter and I feel. It is, after all, nearly midnight, and I fear he put my excitement to an evening of wine."

Peter groaned. "A lot can happen before morning. How about these relatives of yours?"

"Ah, men of the sod!" said Steve.

"Sons of the soil," I murmured.

"The Popodapoulis family have lived in this valley for many generations. They live simply but are good shepherds and understand their goats. Here is my plan." When he described how he proposed to rescue Bart, my hopes rose.

The dark, quiet houses of Kastraki were already around us. Steve drove through the village, turned the van in the road beyond, and coasted downgrade until we were opposite the path Peter and I had used earlier.

He parked well off the road and we climbed out, closing the doors as quietly as possible. The night was still and black as Peter led the way along the path, past sleeping houses to the broken wall where we had spent so many hours.

The cottage below the crumbling shed was only a dark shape. Neither sound nor light showed where it stood, but we had found our night vision and we could make out its silhouette.

"I'll be back in half an hour," whispered Steve. "I'm leaving the rope here, and my old flashlight. Have to take the better one with me." He faded into the night.

We settled ourselves to wait. Although the air was warm and dry, the ground felt damp and the stones, cold. Peter's arm came around my shoulders and he pulled me close. I could read it as a brotherly gesture or as something more. Dear Peter! He was friendly and outgoing but, at the same time, shy and reserved.

"Half an hour isn't very long to wake up a household in the middle of the night and persuade them to help," I whispered. "Do you think Steve's plan will work?"

"It will work all right," Peter breathed in my ear. "I wish I'd thought of it myself."

Time drifted by. The only sounds I could hear were the clickings of night insects and Peter's steady breathing. Then the grass behind us rustled, and Steve squatted next to the wall. He smelled slightly of garlic and goats.

"All set!" he whispered. "When we hear the bells coming up the hill, we will go down and get into position. There will be five men, all brothers, and two dogs with the goats."

Again the night insects took over.

The time passed very slowly. We did not try to talk: the plan was in motion and the important thing now was to remain undiscovered. There was no sign of movement in the house below, but that didn't mean that no one was on guard. A dog barked in the distance and others joined in. Perhaps they were marking the progress of the Popodapoulis brothers.

After a long while, we heard the distant tinkle of the little bells worn by the lead goats. "A few more minutes," murmured Steve.

The tinkling bells drew nearer. We could hear the gruff commands of the shepherds to their dogs, and a feeble lantern light flickered past the first houses in the lane below us.

"Time to move!" said Steve, jumping to his feet.

I stubbed my toe as we crept single file down to

the cottage wall and the high little window. The goats were close by, their sharp bleats mingling with the sounds of the dogs. I knew one Popodapoulis brother would have slipped ahead to keep the goats from passing beyond the cottage.

The light from the lantern had reached the front of the building when we heard the first angry cry from inside.

"The door was open, as we thought!" Steve said, so softly I could barely hear his words. "Those oaths concern awaking in a room full of goats."

A brighter light glowed from the front of the house. Loud voices were raised in argument, goats bleated, and dogs barked.

"Now!" Steve directed. He crouched below the window and Peter stepped onto his shoulder. Peter grabbed the unseen sill and pulled himself part way into the little opening. In a moment, he dropped back.

"There's a bit of light shining through from the front room," he reported. "Bart's on a cot to the left of the window. When you go in, Marty, watch the door and don't let any goats in."

He slipped the end of Steve's coil of rope through his belt and pulled himself up to the window again. As he wriggled through, Steve straightened and held out his hand to me.

I stepped onto Steve's bent knee and he propelled me onto his shoulders. I could just reach the window.

While I pulled, he held me by the knees and lifted me the needed inches so that my elbows were on the sill.

I dug my sneaker toes into the rough stones of the wall and inched my way through the opening. When I was halfway, I stretched out my arms and my hands met Peter's. He grabbed my wrists and pulled gently. With a thud, my feet landed on the dirt floor.

There was a tremendous racket outside the cottage. Greek voices shouted and argued amid frightened goat sounds and the constant barking of the dogs. Certainly no one was paying any attention to this small room.

Bart lay still on the cot in the corner. Peter was already bending over him, slicing at the knotted rope that bound him hand and foot. My father's eyes were wide and gleaming, but an evil-looking rag was pulled tightly across his mouth. The room smelled terrible, an odor of vomit and unwashed humans and worse.

"Watch the door!" Peter said sharply as I started to work on the gag. "We'll get to that in a minute."

I flattened myself against the inner wall and peered cautiously through the opening. Two goats sniffed at scrambled bedrolls on the floor, but the men were outside. I pushed the heavy door shut and leaned against it. The latch was on the other side and there was no way to fasten it from here.

Peter helped Bart sit up and began to rub circulation

into his legs. A sharp hiss sounded through the window.

"Hurry!" Steve called.

Peter wrapped the rope around Bart's chest and over his shoulders. "Use your arms if you can," he whispered. "A man outside will help pull you through."

He put an arm around Bart and eased him to the window. The packed dirt floor came up higher on the inside wall than did the sloping ground outside, and it was not so long a reach to the sill.

Bart got his hands over the edge and Peter pushed him up. But Bart's broad shoulders stuck in the small opening and he wriggled feebly, his feet already a yard above the floor. Steve must have given the rope a mighty yank because Bart suddenly popped on through. I thought of the drop on the outside and prayed that Steve had been able to soften the landing.

Before I could begin to worry, however, Peter was helping me up and over myself. As my stomach slid across the sill, I called softly to Steve. He and Bart seemed to be in a pile on the ground. In the darkness, a figure rose and held out its arms. I dived into them.

The arms tightened. My heart, pounding from the excitement and fear of the rescue, almost exploded with joy as I recognized the familiar clasp. Gagged and groggy though he was, Bart communicated his love and thankfulness through the strength of his hug.

CHAPTER 16

I led Bart up the hill to our protective stone wall. Only then did I start to work on the greasy knot of his gag, prodding carefully in the darkness. I kept up a running whisper, telling him how glad I was to see him and not to worry, all would work out. I don't know what else I said because I was still listening to the racket below the cottage. There was a different tenor to the sounds, an authoritative bark to sharp orders being issued.

Peter appeared at my elbow, his dim flashlight suddenly illuminating Bart's haggard face. "The police came after all! Steve's gone around to see them. Here, let's see if I can cut that thing with my knife."

I sagged against the corner, responsibility slipping away like a hundred-pound load dropping from my shoulders. My hand shook as I held the flashlight for Peter, who gingerly inserted his penknife blade along the back of Bart's neck.

In a moment, the ugly gag fell away. Bart uttered a groan and spit into the weeds. He formed words which made no sound. He tried again. " . . . so good to see you . . . great team you have with you?"

"This is Peter—Peter Muller. You know him," I said over the lump in my throat. "The other one is Steve Nakrodis. He's a friend from Athens. We followed you from Olympia, Bart."

". . . get here? And Peter?" His voice was a scratchy whisper.

"We'll tell you all about it later. I was so scared they would kill you, Bart . . ."

"Marty! Peter!" Steve's strong voice boomed through the darkness. "Come on down here!"

With Bart between us, we picked our way around the cottage. In the front, a remarkable scene was revealed by several glaring spotlights. Only in Greece, I thought as I squinted against the glare.

Goats were everywhere, milling restlessly in and out among five tall, bearded Greeks who wore satisfied smirks on what could be seen of their faces. Two men, huge, bare-chested, and hairy, were handcuffed to equally hefty police officers. Another policeman was just appearing from inside the cottage, a revolver in

147

one hand and a flashlight in the other. A small man in a neat business suit stood apart from the goats, talking to Steve.

Steve turned toward us and extended his hand to Bart. "Mr. Mickelson! I am Stephanos Nakrodis and this is Mr. Mandekos, the head of the police in this district."

Bart shook hands with both men, and Steve translated as the police chief rattled away in Greek.

"He asks that you identify these rascals as your captors. Then he suggests that you—and all of us—accompany him to his office in Kalambaka. He says it will be easier to concentrate without the goats."

"I like a man with a sense of humor," Bart said in a scratchy voice. "Of course I can identify these two men. But there are others, you know."

"Yes, Mr. Mandekos assumed there were. When we reach his office, he wants to hear all that you can tell him. He will leave men here in case the others return tonight."

Steve conferred with Mr. Mandekos again and turned to me. "You may ride into town in the police car with your father. Peter and I will follow with the van. See you very shortly!" He walked away to talk with the Popodapoulis brothers.

Peter stepped close to me and squeezed my arm. "Your father's safe now, Marty," he said softly. In a louder voice, he spoke to Bart. "You don't look too well, sir. Are you able to go on to the chief's office?"

"I'll be all right," Bart replied. "Just need something to drink. I'm so dry. . . . Thanks for everything, Peter."

Mr. Mandekos had sent one of his men to drive a small black sedan to the edge of the milling goats. When Bart and I were settled in its back seat, someone passed in a jug of water and Bart sucked at it thirstily.

As the driver backed from the alley and turned onto the main road, I saw other black vehicles waiting for the officers who had come to our rescue. One looked satisfyingly like a miniature paddy-wagon and would soon be carrying my father's captors away.

The ride to Kalambaka was all too brief. It was like waking from an endless nightmare to have Bart beside me, safe from the gruesome plans of Dr. Nigrita, and I wished we could have spent an hour or more in that cozy little sedan. Since he still spoke with difficulty, I did most of the talking, describing the clues Peter and I had followed as we searched for him. I was anxious to know more about his own investigation, but his hand in mine felt hot and feverish and his words seemed such an effort that I asked none of the questions churning in my mind.

Only when we were unloading at the police headquarters in Kalambaka did I realize how weak Bart was. He let me help him out of the car and leaned heavily on my arm as we entered the building. Slumped on a hard wooden chair under the bright, garish light of the office, he looked yellow and sick. Mr. Mandekos bustled about giving sharp orders to unseen helpers until, at last, Peter and Steve arrived. In the harsh light, they looked crumpled, dirty, and triumphant; I suppose I was the same.

Mr. Mandekos settled behind a bare, uncluttered desk and began to ask questions.

"He would like a full accounting of your kidnapping, Mr. Mickelson," said Steve. "He is very anxious to make further arrests tonight before those involved can scatter."

As in any good police scene, a uniformed man sat in one corner taking notes. Two other officers crowded the doorway, poised to carry out the orders of their chief. I was between Bart and Peter; Steve was close by, poised to act as interpreter.

I felt the effort Bart made as he pulled himself straight in his chair. He began to talk slowly, stopping often to sip from the glass at his elbow. There was quite a selection of beverages on the table now: water, grapefruit juice, and coffee. I welcomed a cup of the steaming brew.

It had all begun a month ago, Bart said, while he was in Athens to set up a new project. Two or three times, Mr. Moskonos had been absent from important conferences, and Mr. Nikolas appeared both surprised and annoyed. Still, Moskonos was a sociable man, so when Bart, looking for an out-of-the-way restaurant one evening, caught sight of his familiar figure, he had hurried to catch up. Perhaps they could eat together, he thought, or, at least, Moskonos would give him better directions.

The banker had entered a dingy taverna with small, filthy windows. Unattractive but not alarming. Bart followed him into a cluttered room, empty except for the men gathered at a table near the door. For a few seconds, a dozen hostile eyes turned toward him; then Moskonos stepped forward, greeting him and drawing him into the group.

"My colleague from the bank," Moskonos had announced smoothly. "Shall we not sell him one of these mementos?"

A small icon was thrust into Bart's hands, one of the five or six spread across the greasy table top. In the harsh light, the Byzantine portraits were strikingly colorful.

Bart grinned at the police chief ruefully. "Even then, they must have known they'd have to get their merchandize back, no matter how. But they wanted to be rid of me as quickly as possible, without arousing my curiosity. At the time they succeeded, and Moskonos ushered me out the door with my purchase and a scribbled receipt. The whole business was over in a matter of minutes, but as I walked away from that odd gathering, my suspicions began. The clutter in the room took on the shape of many wooden crates, and the faces of the men were sly and greedy. I recalled rumors concerning thefts and substitutions in the art world, and a vague, ugly possibility began to haunt me. Was Moskonos mixed up in something illegal? The integrity of my bank could be seriously affected if any of its officers were involved in shady schemes. I only wondered then—now, unfortunately, I know it's true."

Bart paused and sipped more water. Then he told of the next day at the bank, a busy one with no chance to speak privately with Moskonos about the encounter. Beginning to feel ill, he had returned early to his room and sensed at once that his clothes had been disturbed. Nothing missing—simply evidence of someone's hasty search. But other than thievery, what could have been the motive? The icon, purchased under bizarre circumstances, came immediately to mind. It had been traveling in his briefcase, always at his side. Now he studied it more closely: very beautiful, with such fine craftsmanship that it could possibly be more than a well-executed reproduction.

He'd wondered since if his illness—cough, cold, fever, too, no doubt—had clouded his judgment. Wrapping the icon carefully, he tucked it beneath a scarf he'd already chosen for my birthday present and, in the morning, sent the package on its way. For customs, he declared the prices of the gifts as shown on his receipts.

Entering the bank that day, he passed Mr. Moskonos talking to a tall, bald-headed man who'd been at the taverna. Bart caught a word or two of their low-voiced conversation: "Lisbon" and "shipment" were the most distinct. Once in the office upstairs, those words made him quick to notice a list of addresses lying on Moskonos' desk—a list not on bank stationery. He'd just noted an entry for Portugal when Moskonos himself came in, picked up the paper, and stuffed it in a drawer.

Bart continued to feel worse all day but, even so, he decided to take a week's leave—he'd go to Lisbon himself and investigate. Then, perhaps, if he wasn't over his wretched cold, he could spend a few days in Lucerne with the Mullers.

He advised Mr. Moskonos of his plans, without mentioning Lisbon, of course, and asked Moskonos to notify all the proper persons about his leave.

I exchanged a triumphant glance with Peter. We had been right about Mr. Moskonos and his lies all along.

That night Bart flew to Portugal. His condition worsened on the plane, and he collapsed as he disembarked. An ambulance had whisked him to the hospital.

He woke up in Santa Luzia. When he was a little better, he'd sent cables to Mr. Nikolas and me, scribbling his messages word by painful word and hoping the nurse would get it straight.

"She didn't," I interrupted. "I thought, when the

153

cable came, it said you needed 'Two Bart.' But later I found the letter you dropped and saw you had not meant that at all."

Bart smiled at me fondly. "Much as I might have wanted you, it didn't occur to me to ask you to come to Lisbon—we have a helpful Portuguese nurse to thank for that."

He was still very weak when he persuaded the doctors he could leave the hospital. He went at once to the address he'd seen in Athens, but it was only a deserted building along the Lisbon waterfront. Any vessel discharging or taking on cargo had long since departed—still, a shipment *could* have passed through there. It had seemed imperative to return to Greece at once so, after stopping at American Express, he boarded a late afternoon flight. As he flew, he scrawled a note to the Mullers and then composed a more thoughtful letter to me.

He had intended to speak first to Mr. Nikolas and then report his suspicions to the authorities. On the Friday he returned to the bank, however, he'd had no opportunity to see Nikolas alone. Leaving my letter, he arranged a private meeting on the following morning, but it was an appointment he never kept. In bright sunlight, surrounded by crowds of hurrying shoppers, he'd felt the prick of a needle, a man grasping his arm, and then—nothing. He had only a few disjointed memories of what followed—a boat, a wooden house

on an island—a tiny room behind an artist's studio—
days of nothing, of foggy thoughts—of someone
spooning soup between his lips. He knew now that
one of Dr. Nigrita's band of icon artists had been his
jailer. The only name he heard was "Milo"—perhaps
a code since it means "apple" in Greek.

Four or five days later, he'd been transported again
and, groggy but upright on his own feet, he'd been
led into the Olympic grounds. There, he had caught
a glimpse of Moskonos and, for the first time, had
seen the ringleader. Dr. Nigrita had appeared very angry because Olympia was the only meeting place to
which Milo would agree. The artist had traveled with
a backpack he'd guarded more diligently even than
his prisoner, and Bart had understood enough to realize
it contained new icons to replace those the thieves
were about to steal from the monasteries.

The gang, all dressed in their city business suits,
had gone off with the stubborn artist, leaving him with
a single guard beside the source of the Olympian flame.
The guard later permitted him to rest in the passage
to the playing fields, and it was then he traced his
name on the stones. A despairing hope that someone
might notice and ask questions.

Bart looked at me. "And someone did. My daughter!"

He said the fresh air had revived him further. When
he saw his watchman dozing in the sun, he tiptoed

away, managing to find a telephone kiosk outside the entrance. He'd made the call to Switzerland and the Mullers because, his brain still clouded, theirs was the only number he could remember. Before he'd spoken more than a few words, however, he'd been yanked away and thrust into a nearby car. In the hotel parking lot, with an almost invisible tape over a gag, they'd dragged him out and walked him into the hotel itself. Left locked in a room alone, he had managed to get his fingers into a small pocket inside another pocket and pulled out Marty's letter, which they had missed when they searched him. Once on the floor, a lot of footwork got the paper into his loafer. It was all he had to use as a clue.

Then the men returned and a needle had sent him into oblivion again, More time passed. When they dragged him to the car, all he could do was kick off his shoe and hope. In the dank little room where they'd found him tonight, the drugs had begun to wear off. He hadn't known he was in Kastraki, but he'd listened to familiar voices in the room beyond. Two more icons had been stolen from the monasteries, and a courier would pick them up tomorrow. Another shipment of art treasures was due at the same time, to be loaded on a large fishing boat docked at Itea, the little harbor Peter and I had thought so charming. Mr. Moskonos was supplying stamps and papers which would make it look as though the crates had already cleared Greek Customs.

Bart's voice was becoming very weak. "I don't think he can talk much more," I said. "Can't we get him to bed now? Please?"

Mr. Mandekos was human after all. He smiled at me and nodded. It was agreed that Peter would go with the police to identify Dr. Nigrita and his cohorts while Steve and I took Bart to the Argos Hotel. In the morning, a doctor would be around to see how he was feeling. "In the morning"! The hour was already three o'clock, and I thought bed sounded pretty great myself.

CHAPTER 17

It was noon on Wednesday when Peter, Steve, and I gathered in the little bakery for a late breakfast. Peter and Steve had been up for less than an hour, neither having turned in until daybreak. I'd slept a little and was ready to meet the doctor when he came to examine Bart.

The doctor's English had been hard to follow, but he assured me that Bart's condition wasn't serious. The pneumonia had not returned, and the abrasions from the ropes that had bound his hands and feet would heal quickly. His cut lips, where the gag had pulled ruthlessly at the corners of his mouth, would be painful for a little longer. A few days' rest, and my father should be as good as new.

Peter and Steve were full of their part in the police activities. "We got them all out of bed!" Peter exclaimed. "Dr. Nigrita was a name-caller. Said he knew everyone from the Premier on down . . . "

"Name-dropper, I'll bet," I said.

"The others, that bald-headed man and the Englishman, Thomas, were just glum. They didn't have more than three words to say the whole time."

"They did admit they were to meet a truck in Kastraki this morning," Steve added. "Mr. Mandekos has sent some of his own men in their place."

"Dr. Nigrita and Mr. Moskonos won't get off lightly," Peter continued. "They knew the law—it's almost a mortal sin to send art treasures out of the country without a government permit."

"As it should be," said Steve, licking his fingers. "Too many of our Greek and Roman antiquities have gone, and Byzantine art is also a valuable part of our past."

I had to interrupt. "Time to go wake Bart for lunch," I said as I slid along the bench and stood up. "You're both to come. He's anxious to see you again."

We returned to Athens the following morning, Steve's van providing a comfortable couch on which Bart traveled. For two days, we stayed at a hotel outside the city, a big airy place with a shady terrace where my father spent much of his time.

When we weren't with Bart, Peter and I roamed the grounds and talked without interruption until, to my private dismay, the day of departure arrived. My flight left only an hour ahead of the one carrying Peter to Zurich. Bart escorted us to the airport, and there I parted from the two most important people in my life.

Belted into my high-backed seat, I felt the big plane rise smoothly into the clear Greek skies. Below, Athens sprawled across its hills like a humped mural of some make-believe city, but I barely noticed. My senses were numb with the emotions of the past half-hour.

Bart had promised he'd be home for my graduation. "The conference in Vienna will be over," he said, smiling, "and nothing in the world can keep me away—not even kidnappers!"

Then Peter had gathered me into his arms and whispered, "'Til next fall, Marty! I'm coming to your country then—" and he named the very college Bart had helped me choose. There was nothing brotherly about the kiss that followed and, in a happy daze, I'd joined the line of boarding passengers.

Now I unwrapped the little package Peter had pushed into my hand. Without looking, I knew what it contained. An icon. Inside would be the painted pictures—of whom, it didn't matter. Just the feel of the smooth wooden covers was enough, that and the memory of his parting kiss.